Y0-EKP-417

THE WEDDING TOAST

Regina Duke

PUBLISHED BY:
RD Books, Sparks, NV

The Wedding Toast
Copyright © 2016 Linda White; 2017 paperback

Publisher's Cataloging-in-Publication data

Names: Duke, Regina, author.
Title: The wedding toast / Regina Duke.
Series: Colorado Billionaires.
Description: Sparks, NV : RD Books, 2017.
Identifiers: ISBN 978-1-944752-07-1 (pbk.) | 978-0-9862903-4-3
(ebook) | LCCN 2017944682
Subjects: LCSH Man-woman relationships--Fiction. | Life change
events--Fiction. | Colorado--Fiction. | Ranch -- Fiction. | Rich people--
Fiction. | Romance--Fiction. | Love stories. | Romantic stories. |
BISAC FICTION / Romance / Contemporary. | FICTION /
Contemporary Women.
Classification: LCC PS3604.U43T63 2017 | DDC 813.6--dc23

Print ISBN: 978-1-944752-07-1
Ebook ISBN: 978-0-9862903-4-3
Library of Congress Control Number: 2017944682

ALL RIGHTS RESERVED. With the exception of quotes used in
reviews, this book may not be reproduced or used in whole or in part by
any means existing without written permission from Regina Duke.

This book is a work of fiction and all characters exist solely in the
author's imagination. Any resemblance to persons, living or dead, is
purely coincidental. Any references to places, events or locales are used
in a fictitious manner.

Edited by Marian Kelly
Formatting by StevieDeInk
Cover design by StevieDeInk
Cover photos from Fotolia.com

Chapter One

Tuesday, April 4

"BUT MISS HAZEN, YOUR father is on a conference call!"

Too late. Taylor Hazen ignored her father's secretary and headed for the double oak doors of his plush Lower Manhattan office. After all, she had been summoned.

Taylor threw both doors open and headed straight for his ebony desk. She was the only person in the company who dared to approach Pembroke Hazen without an appointment.

Taylor stood there, arms crossed, chin up, and her shapely legs planted as firmly on the thick carpet as her Jimmy Choo's would allow. The black skirt of her designer suit was stretched as tight as her expression. Her stylish blue bob matched the color of her eyes. She didn't say a word. She just glared at her father.

Pembroke's steel-gray hair was as abundant as it had been in his twenties, and his eyes were the same color as his hair. His conversation didn't miss a beat as his daughter strode into his office.

Taylor stood still for as long as she could. She knew her father was dragging the call out, just to annoy her. At last, she began to pace, with the hope that her movement would irritate him into cutting the call short. The floor-to-ceiling glass provided an amazing view of the New York City skyline, and she was drawn to it as if against her will.

Jackson was out there, waiting for her. Jackson, her one true friend. They'd practically grown up together. But instead of cleaning tack and

3

riding in Central Park, she was forced to labor in the mailroom of the family enterprise. She caught a glimmer of her own reflection in the glass and ran a hand through her blue-tinted hair. Her father's change of tone shattered her reverie.

"Don't just stand there looking at the scenery. Come have a seat."

Taylor turned but stayed where she was. Her voice dripped sarcasm. "Are you sure I have time? After all, I have such important duties in the mailroom. Whatever will I tell my supervisor?"

Pembroke spoke sternly but his eyes twinkled. "Get off that high horse of yours or I'll send you back down right now." He motioned toward one of the cream-colored leather chairs that faced his desk.

Taylor surrendered and did as he asked. "Really, Daddy, the mailroom? I know you want me to learn the business from the ground up, but this is ridiculous. It's bleak and dusty, and no one wants to talk to me."

"That's because you walk in there dressed like a female tycoon and you take every opportunity to remind them you're my daughter. Exactly the opposite of what I asked you to do. As for bleak and dusty, please spare me. Everything down there is state of the art."

Taylor made an exasperated noise. If only her father would cater to her every whim, the way he used to do when she was little. But ever since high school, when she started looking more like a woman than a little girl, she felt he'd hardened toward her. As a result, she found herself assuming a flippant attitude whenever they talked. "Did my brothers have to play this silly game? Did they have to start at the bottom of the ladder?"

"Never mind about your brothers. Don's been paying his dues in the San Francisco office for two years. Longer, if we count his college internship. Young Greg is still at prep school, but he's already giving serious thought to how he can contribute to the family business. And Bart...well, we both know Bart's a lost cause. Let him stay in Paris and paint. When he realizes he's going to need a real job, he'll come crawling back."

Taylor crossed her legs, twining them, with the toe of her right shoe behind her left heel. Girded for battle.

Pembroke gestured with one hand. "How on Earth do you do that? Oh, to be young again."

Taylor relaxed her posture and uncrossed her legs. Leave it to Daddy to play the age card. She slanted her knees to one side. "Sorry, Daddy. You're not exactly old yourself."

"Older than you know. Too old to have my only daughter practically put on boxing gloves every time I call her into my office." He stood up and turned to stare at the skyline, hands folded behind his back. "I put you in the mailroom because I need someone I can trust keeping an eye out and an ear to the ground for me. Not because I think you need to spend your youth learning to sort packages."

Taylor wondered how much of that was the truth and how much was him trying to get on her good side so she'd do what he wanted. But what the heck, he was her father. He held the purse strings. She used to have more sway with him than her brothers did. But even then, she always complied with his wishes. She leaned her head against the back of the chair and asked, "What do you want me to do?"

Pembroke turned, all smiles. "That's my girl. I knew I could count on you." He returned to his chair, serious again. "I've been working on a complicated deal with Lester Garrison. Did I tell you about Garrison?"

"It's all you've talked about for months," said Taylor, making a face. "You play golf with him, right? Why isn't he putty in your hands?"

"It's a long story, but I think you can help me swing this deal. And if you do, I'll make you a vice president. How's that sound?"

Taylor sat bolt upright. "Seriously?"

"I thought that might get your attention." Pembroke opened a drawer and withdrew a folder with the Hazen logo on it. "It turns out, Lester has a son out in Colorado who fancies himself a writer." He snorted. "I guess every family has a Bart, eh?"

Taylor frowned. She considered her brother a great artist in the making, but she'd been down that road before with her father, and it never ended well, so instead she said, "I thought the Colorado Garrisons were Rudy's family."

Pembroke waved away the mention of Rudy Garrison as if it were a fly. "Rooster's too busy playing with his money over in Kuwait, or wherever the heck he is this month. As for Lester, if we'd done this deal three years ago, we'd have been finished lickety-split. But he changed after his wife died. Found himself a runway model. I think he's getting senile. His kids are not pleased about it, either. And his oldest has taken off to Colorado to put some distance between himself and his father, and to play at being a writer."

Taylor leaned forward, elbows on the arms of the chair, fingers laced together. "When do we get to the part you want me to play in all of this?"

Pembroke tapped a bony finger on the file. "I've arranged for you to go out west and dig up some dirt on Lester Garrison."

Taylor was confused. "But he's in New York."

"I know. But his son is writing Lester's biography, and I've arranged for you to be his personal editor on this project. He'll write about his old man, you'll ask keen and penetrating questions, and before you know it, we'll have plenty of leverage to use on Lester."

Taylor's eyes narrowed. "You want me to dig up dirt so you can blackmail Lester into agreeing to your terms in the deal you're working on?"

Pembroke leaned back in his chair and grinned. He was at the age where it sometimes looked like his teeth were too big for his mouth. And never more so than now, as he contemplated besting Lester Garrison in a business deal. He looked like a wolf drooling over a sheep.

"How long will I have to maintain this charade?" Taylor thought at once of how much she would miss Jackson.

"That depends on how long it takes to win Axel's confidence and get me some useful information. Everything you need is in here. You'll fly on the company jet. There'll be a rental car waiting for you." He slid the folder across his desk. "I wanted to put a map in here, but my secretary told me you kids all use GPS, so…." He shrugged.

Taylor reached for the folder. She peeked inside. Her father had provided her with a report on Garrison industries and a salary schedule for Hazen executives. Her eyes locked onto that right away. Maybe this errand wouldn't be too horrible after all. At least she'd have something pleasant to think about. "When I get back, I'm a vice president?"

"Once the deal is complete."

Taylor pinned her father with a knowing look. "Not good enough. Deals and mergers can fall through. When I get back, I get my own office with a nice view of Manhattan, my own secretary, and an upper management position to tide me over until the deal is done. Once that happens, I'll be happy to move into my new position as a vice president."

Pembroke threw his head back and laughed. "Taylor, my dear, you are a chip off the old block. It's a deal. Now go home and pack. You leave first thing in the morning."

Taylor hugged the folder to her chest as she left the office. On her way down to the mailroom to collect her purse, a smile took hold of her. Vice president. Of what? It didn't matter. Taylor Hazen, VP of Whatever, with a seven-figure salary that would let her take care of Jackson in spectacular style. She could hardly wait. She punched the elevator button and giggled like a school girl. "Look out, Axel Garrison. Here I come." She patted the folder. "Poor guy. He's not going to know what hit him."

Chapter Two

Wednesday, April 6

AXEL GARRISON LEFT THE TOWN council meeting halfway through, shaking his head in disgust. Then he glanced around to make sure his cousin Thor hadn't seen his reaction to the heated discussion he'd witnessed. What a waste of a beautiful day. It was already three o'clock. The air was fresh and clean, recently washed by an April shower that was more like a downpour. He splashed through a puddle at the foot of the town hall steps. It felt later than three because of the cloud cover. The weather had more in store.

Until people heard his last name, they didn't know he was related to his Norse-like cousins. They were all blond and blue-eyed. He was brunet and brown-eyed, like his mother. Rudy and Lester Garrison, his uncle and father respectively, had chosen very different mothers for their children.

He snorted softly as he got into his mud-spattered Ford Expedition. The thought of his father's second wife elicited an intense revulsion in him, as it did in his siblings. After their mother died three years ago, Lester Garrison seemed to go off the deep end. Everyone understood his grief. What they couldn't understand was his pursuant marriage to Bambi, the runway model. She was the same age as Axel, and that creeped him out.

Their incomprehensible relationship was the reason he'd decided to try the fresher air in Colorado. He couldn't stand to watch Bambi fawn

7

all over his father whenever Lester was in the room, then go about the business of spending his money when he wasn't. None of Axel's siblings had managed to get through to his father about the possibility of her being a gold digger, and when Axel took a turn at reasoning with his old man, sparks flew. Lester had lost his temper, and Axel met his father's anger with some temper of his own.

On top of that, just last November, his father had had the audacity to announce at the Forbes wedding that Axel would be the next in their group to walk down the aisle. Axel remembered cringing as his father slurred out his toast.

"Here's to the bride and groom," he'd said, raising his glass. "Ray, you're a fine man, but not even you deserve a bride as beautiful as Maria. May you both live forever and have ten children. And speaking of children, it's about time my lot started to settle down. I make a toast to Ray and Maria, and I make a promise, that my oldest will marry within a year! Cheers!"

The argument that had ensued on the drive home after the wedding had been monumental. No voices were raised. That wasn't Lester's style. But he could pack more menace and aggravation into a quiet sentence than any man alive, and by God, he wanted grandchildren! When Axel had snidely suggested that he and Bambi make their own, Lester's response had been pointed and cold.

"I've made a huge investment in your education, and you fritter it all away on this daydream of being a writer. For God's sake, at least do something that will bring in some cash. And if you can't do that, then make me some grandkids. Maybe success skips a generation."

The result was Axel's decision that they needed space if they were ever going to get to a point where they could have a civil conversation again. Axel didn't want to lose contact completely. He loved his father, and Lester's scathing words had hurt him deeply. How could he rave on about how important money was when he'd complained for years that it was all his brother Rudy valued in life?

Eventually Axel realized the wedding toast was also part of his father's competition with Rudy. Thor and Ulysses Garrison, Rudy's sons, were already married, and Thor even had two kids for Rudy to bounce on his knee.

Well, Axel wasn't about to get married just to puff up his father's ego. Besides, he had four siblings—Tony, Dustin, Andrea, and Katie. Let them have kids!

He felt a twinge of guilt as he recalled Lester's brush with ill health.

There had been some scary moments after Axel's mother died. Lester had suffered from a major depression before he married Bambi. Could his father be worried that he might not live to see his grandchildren? Axel brushed that off. Lester was probably fine. If something were wrong, surely he would have confided in one of the girls. Either way, it wasn't doing them any good to fight over that stupid toast.

So Axel took a trip to Colorado to see his cousins. The next thing he knew, he was buying property and loving the view. He'd already written half his novel since arriving in Eagle's Toe. It was also a relief not to have to talk to his father every day. A little silence, he figured, would be golden. And his plan was working. Their conversation the week before had been almost cordial.

"Axel, it's Dad."

The phone call had come out of the blue, and Axel's response was instinctive. "Is everything okay?"

"It's fine," said Lester. "I figured I better call, because if I wait for your apology, we might never talk again."

Axel knew that those words were the closest he would ever get to hearing his father say he was sorry. They'd exchanged some hurtful words during that last fight. Still, he was cautious. "Okay, Dad. I acknowledge that we are equally stubborn. What's up?"

Lester sighed heavily. "Well, son, I'm not getting any younger, you know. And none of us lasts forever."

Alarm bells went off for Axel. He'd never known his father to admit his own mortality. Maybe something *was* going on that he didn't know about. "Dad, are you all right?"

"I'm fine, I'm fine."

To Axel's ear, it sounded like his father was trying very hard to convince him that all was well. "Would you tell me if something was wrong?"

Lester's temper flared. "Can't a man talk to his oldest son without a visit to the Mayo Clinic?"

Axel relaxed. That was more like it. "Of course, Dad. I just.... We may argue, but you know I love you. Most of the time."

Lester laughed, a rough hacking sound. "That's why I wanted to say, ah, well...oh, dang it all, when I told you it was foolish of you to waste time trying to be a writer, I was taking a cheap shot. I know you have talent. In fact, I want you to write my life story."

Axel wasn't sure he was hearing correctly. "Your biography? Really? Are you sure you're okay?"

"Yes, I'm sure. I just saw my doctor, and I've got lots of time. Hell, I'm only in my fifties, boy."

Axel couldn't help but smile. His father's Texas roots were shining through again. He knew he couldn't refuse Lester's request. This was his chance to bury the hatchet with his father. But his novel would not be done by the end of the year if he started another project. He took half a second to weigh the novel against winning his father's favor again, and family won.

"I can do it, Dad. I should have a first draft for you in about twelve months."

"I need it by Christmas."

"It's already April, Dad. That doesn't seem possible. I'd have to work nonstop on it for the next eight months."

"I know, I know. It's an imposition, but I want to surprise the family with a nice bound book about the story of my life. Roots are important. And by the time you tell my story, you'll be telling your mother's story as well. She was a huge part of me, remember?"

That did it. Axel knew he had to say yes. He suspected the whole project was a roundabout way of saying Lester wanted him to write a tribute to his late mother. "I'll do it, Dad. But Christmas?" He did some mental calculations. "I'll have to get it to a printer by the end of October, and before that, the editing process.... I just don't know how I'll be able to get it all done."

"I know I'm asking a lot," said Lester. "That's why I'm sending you an assistant. Name is Taylor. Lots of editorial experience. Great resume. You can dictate your memories of me. It'll go real fast that way. Taylor will do all the editing as you go."

Axel didn't have the heart to tell his father it didn't really work that way. It was obvious the old man was passionate about the project. "Okay, Dad. I'll do it."

"Good. Great. Taylor will arrive next week. I made a reservation at that Cattleman's Inn, the one your cousins told us about. How are they doing?"

"They're fine. Uly and Belle fly back and forth between here and Las Vegas. They're buying property down there, and Belle is helping Lulamae. Why didn't you tell me my godmother had a hip replaced? And Thor is all wrapped up in some power struggle with the town council and the local Grange. Seems the town folk and ranchers around here aren't thrilled about his plans for luxury housing."

"Well, he'll work it out somehow. Okay, son, you take care. I'm late for a meeting. You get started on my book now, you hear me?"

The memory of that phone call nagged at Axel as he drove slowly through Eagle's Toe. He'd have to alert his siblings to keep an eye out for health problems in Lester. On the other hand, if it was a sneaky way to honor their late mother, Axel was all for it. He could imagine the looks on their faces when they each received a bound volume of their parents' life stories. He checked his dashboard display. He'd spent the last week getting things organized in the rustic cabin on his property. His new barn was up and his fences were good. He was having a large house built, but the builders had barely gotten started on the foundation. After a few months of living at the Cattleman's, he was ready for the privacy afforded by the cabin, but it had taken time to get it livable. Meanwhile, he'd been driving back and forth in the snow and mud since February, feeding his livestock and supervising the construction projects.

And in the week since his father's call, he'd decided that the cabin would be the perfect place to work uninterrupted. He could turn off his cell and ignore all the distractions of living in town. It would be a writer's paradise. Having an assistant would work out just fine. In fact, once the weather warmed up, he could dictate while fishing. He had a great bass pond on his property.

He smirked. He hadn't bothered to tell his father that his purchase of eighty acres had landed him smack dab in the middle of his cousin's fight with the locals. And the last time he'd talked to Thor—a few days before the town council meeting—his cousin had let slip that Rudy was also interested in his plans for their Colorado real estate. Axel shook his head. What a combination. Thor and Uncle Rudy. A tiny doubt flitted about his mind like a pesky gnat. Rudy had been an oilman all his life, and Axel couldn't quite wrap his mind around his uncle as a real estate developer.

Neither could he understand why Thor wanted to build luxury homes on land where people had fished and hunted for hundreds of years. Not that Axel wanted to hunt. But the bass pond had sealed the deal, and he couldn't wait to get back to the cabin. He'd bundle up against the April chill, row out to the middle of the pond and throw a line in.

But first, he had to stop at the Cattleman's and pick up his takeout from Il Vaccaro, the Italian restaurant. And he'd better leave a message at the front desk for his new assistant. He was arriving today. What was his name again? Taylor? That was it. He hoped Taylor liked fishing.

Chapter Three

TAYLOR HATED FISH. HOW could the company chef serve her salmon on her flight? She knew she'd hurt his feelings when she requested a peanut butter and jelly sandwich instead. And she knew she'd been snarky. A part of her regretted that. Normally, she was much nicer to employees. But lately, laboring in the mailroom thanks to her father, she'd felt as lowly as they must feel.

She shuddered at the memory. Never again. She deserved a better job than that. And then, to find out he hadn't even expect her to actually do the work, he'd just wanted her to spy for him? In truth, she didn't mind that part. The idea of a little espionage had sounded like fun. She steered her rental car easily around a massive cattle truck. It was disheartening to find she had to drive herself around, but a chauffeur and a limo would blow her cover. The smell of cow manure wrinkled her nose. She turned up the heater. As she rose in altitude, the temperature dropped.

So all she had to do to earn a vice presidency was get some dirt on Lester Garrison. She was ready. Ready for the salary and the corner office, that is. She'd figure out the job. That part didn't matter. That's why people had staff, right? She would have secretaries and middle managers and all those other people who knew what they were doing, and they would all report to her, and she would lean back in her cushy office chair and assign projects. Her father would want quarterly reports. She would choose her best people for those. She'd want her father to be proud of her work.

Okay, maybe proud of her managing skills. Whatever. Wasn't that what she'd heard him telling her brother Don over the phone? She clucked with disgust at the memory. All the praise in the world for Don. Taylor didn't get it. Don told her he was working sixteen-hour days, trying to whip the San Francisco office into shape. Good grief! Didn't he know how to delegate?

Well, she planned to do plenty of delegating. And she could spend her weekends with Jackson. That put a smile on her face. Maybe she could even leave early on Wednesdays, like her father did, and spend those afternoons with Jackson, too. Her forehead crinkled. Technically, her father was still working, making deals, and conducting conference calls from the golf course. She never understood his obsession with golf. Couldn't he do his business deals over lunch? She decided it was a guy thing. After all, men liked sports, and most of the businessmen her father consorted with were too old to play anything else. She wondered if she'd have to take golf lessons once she was a vice president.

The GPS system in her car directed her easily to the Cattleman's Inn. Part of the place was only a few stories high, but at the west end, there was a tower. She definitely wanted to stay in the tower, because it looked new. She cringed at the thought of finding herself in a grungy motel room. She pulled up to the front doors, under the broad portico, and felt a small satisfaction as a bellboy emerged at once with a trolley for her luggage. She checked her hair and makeup, then got out of the car.

As the bellboy loaded the luggage from her trunk, Taylor asked, "Where's the valet?"

The young man looked confused. "Pardon me?"

Taylor quashed the annoyance that simmered just beneath the surface. "The parking valet?" She dangled her car keys off one finger.

"Oh, sorry, ma'am." He seemed fascinated by her blue hair. Didn't these people have hair salons? "We only have valet parking for special events. I'll take these bags to the front desk for you, and once you check in, I'll bring them up to your room, if you like. But you'll have to move your car around to the parking lot."

Taylor closed her fist around her keys. "Gee. Special events. Like the high school prom?"

Her sarcasm was lost on the bellboy. "Mostly weddings and concerts and big charity events and private parties." Without further ado, he closed the trunk and started toward the door.

"Wait! There's more in the back seat."

His glance at the luggage trolley made it clear that he thought two large suitcases and a garment bag were sufficient. But he opened the car door and retrieved two more suitcases and an overnight case. "Is this all, ma'am?"

Taylor tried to read something into his question, but she couldn't. She doubted he was capable of hidden meanings. She tucked her handbag under one arm and headed for the lobby while casting a scathing glance over her shoulder at the bellboy. "I may be here a while," she said.

She tossed her head toward the door, but her eyes were still on the bellboy. She didn't see the man coming out in time to avoid a collision. He was carrying a large white takeout sack and a tall covered drink, and when they collided, the lid came off and the icy cola sloshed all over Taylor's Armani blouse.

With a shriek, she jumped backward, but too late. "Look what you've done! You clumsy jerk!" Her handbag fell to the ground.

The man was tall, broad-shouldered, and wore casual but expensive clothes. Taylor recognized quality when she saw it, and everything about him screamed excellence. But that didn't take the edge off her anger.

"I'm sorry about that," he said calmly, "but you might want to watch where you're going."

"Are you saying this is my fault?" She glared at him. "This blouse is an Armani original, and now it's ruined." She planted her fists on her hips. "What are you going to do about this?"

He looked her up and down, and Taylor felt her cheeks warming beneath his gaze. She could see the glint of amusement in his eyes, and that just made her madder.

"This is not funny," she snapped.

"That depends on your point of view." He had a deep, rich voice that, under different circumstances, Taylor would have found appealing.

A second bellboy appeared on the run, bringing a white towel for Taylor to dry off with. Then he busied himself by helping the first young man push the luggage trolley.

Taylor dabbed at her ruined blouse, still fuming. "My favorite blouse is a total loss and you're making fun of me."

"Not at all. I can tell it's your favorite because you died your hair to match it." He tucked his takeout under one arm and retrieved her handbag for her. "I, on the other hand, may die of thirst." He rattled the remaining ice in his cup.

"Oh, very funny." She took her bag without thanking him, and still dabbing at her blouse, she said, "I suppose you're a native of this quaint little burg."

"I have eighty acres a little way from here, so I qualify as a resident at the very least."

Taylor felt her features pinch with aggravation. Was he still staring at her? If so, it wasn't her hair he was looking at. She cocked a hip at him and gave him her harshest look, the one that said, "Out of my way, peasant."

"Lucky for you," she said aloud, "I'm too busy to pursue this matter." With that, she left him in the portico, too insignificant to interfere with her rise to company vice president. Some day, when she was able to hire and fire people, she'd offer this yokel a huge salary, and then, just when he was thinking he could afford a new tractor, she'd fire him. Just like that. The thought put a smile on her face as she approached the registration desk, still clutching the damp towel to her chest.

A middle-aged man who'd never missed a meal raised bushy eyebrows at her approach. "Everything all right, miss?"

Taylor huffed and looked skyward, like a woman who had tolerated the very last straw. Then she replied, "It will be, someday soon." Silently, she added, *When I have my revenge.*

Chapter Four

AXEL DIDN'T BOTHER TO REFILL his cola. He'd make coffee at the cabin. He'd need to fill a thermos anyway if he was going to spend a few hours on the pond. He wanted to be fishing by four. He couldn't help smiling as he got into his Expedition. The girl with the blue hair certainly had fire in her blood. And the stack of luggage she'd brought? Enough for a year. Maybe he'd run into her again when he came into town in the morning to pick up his new editor-slash-assistant.

He wondered why on Earth he thought it would be pleasant to run into that spitfire again. He shook his head in amazement. Well, she was attractive. Couldn't be more than five feet tall in her bare feet. That must be the reason for the flamboyant hair. She was trying to make up for her lack of inches. Then he laughed out loud as he remembered the look on her face when his cold drink hit her blouse. And he remembered the two perfect mounds beneath the wet fabric.

"Axel, you have been alone too long if you are daydreaming about a handful like her," he scolded himself. "She's going to make some man very miserable some day. Danger, danger, Texas Ranger." That phrase made him think of his father, and he spent the rest of the drive musing about the man's health.

By the time he filled his thermos for fishing, he'd decided to call one of his brothers in the morning to touch base and see if he'd noticed any changes in Lester. Was Tony back from his ski rebellion in the Alps yet? Maybe he'd call Dustin. That made more sense, since Dustin was working in the financial district and saw their father all the time. The twins, Katie and Andrea, were still at MIT and only twenty. They were too young to worry about Lester's possible health issues. They were great at spotting that kind of subtle transformation, but he couldn't lay that worry at their doorstep. Dustin was the only one Lester might confide in about seeing a doctor, since he was twenty-four and actually pursuing the career path Lester had laid out for him. Yes, he'd check in with Dustin.

♡

Taylor was surprised by the luxury of her suite. She never expected an establishment in a small town like Eagle's Toe to understand the concept of true luxury. Of course, it wasn't the Bahamas or the French Riviera, but it was more than acceptable. The colors were drawn from nature, granite and sand with soft blues and greens. And it was roomy, with a wall of windows that looked west to the mountains and Gunnison, a ski resort, according to the brochure she found on the formal conference table at one end of the long living room. At the other end, sand-colored sofas formed a horseshoe that allowed her to enjoy the view no matter where she was seated. In between, there was a bar and an entertainment center. She'd already explored the bedroom, a mini-suite unto itself with two baths, a sleeping area, and a quiet work station tucked into one corner. The perfect hotel suite for a couple who weren't talking to each other.

After changing into jeans and a long-sleeved fleece—the wall of windows made her feel chilly—she helped herself to a diet Pepsi from the bar and plopped down on the middle sofa to stare at the scenery. The sun was setting, and just as the glare became annoying, she heard a whirring sound, and a sunscreen closed softly over the windows. She could still enjoy the view, but the sun's power was reduced. Even so, she got up and pulled the drapes, just far enough to block Old Sol, at least until he slid behind the mountains.

She checked her phone for messages. Nothing. She blew air between her lips, imitating Jackson in a moment of frustration, and leaned her head back on the cushion. "Daddy, you'd better make billions on this deal, because I am stuck in the middle of nowhere to do you this favor."

She thought about going down for dinner or taking a walk around town, but she knew if she did, she would feel better, and she wasn't in the mood to feel better. She wanted to wallow in a pool of self-pity. At least until she recovered from her trip a bit.

Her cell phone played the first four notes of Beethoven's Fifth Symphony. She picked it up. "Hello, Daddy. I was just thinking about you."

He laughed. "I bet you were. How is Eagle's Toe?"

"I haven't seen any of it yet. Just got here. You are going to owe me big time. This place doesn't even have valet parking."

"Keep your eyes on the prize, my girl."

"Corner office?"

"I'm the one with the corner office, remember? How about an unobstructed view of the Manhattan skyline?"

Taylor sighed petulantly. "Oh, all right. I guess that will have to do. How is that deal coming?"

"Having you in Colorado is helping. Lester Garrison thinks I'm doing him a favor by sending you out to help his son write a book. He's softening up."

"Thank goodness! You let me know as soon as he agrees to your terms so I can get back to civilization. How's Jackson?"

"You've been gone one day, Taylor. I haven't had a chance to check on him, but I'm sure he's fine. We pay enough to have people take care of him. Now, have you met this Axelrod yet?"

"Ew, is that his first name? No, not yet. But he left me a note at the registration desk. Signed it 'Garrison.' He says he'll pick me up in the morning and show me how to get to his place. Dad, it's a lot colder here than New York."

"There's a ski resort not far from you, so I suppose their cold weather lasts longer. Go buy yourself a down jacket. Now remember, I need you to spend enough time with this young man to dig up something really good. You got that?"

"I'll do my part. And in my free time, I'll be cruising the internet, looking for office furniture."

He laughed. "You do that. I have to go. Check in every day. Sooner if you learn something really juicy."

"Bye, Daddy."

♡

Pembroke Hazen leaned back in his big chair and swiveled it slowly to and fro. The intercom on his desk pinged softly.

"Mr. Hazen, I've reached that party you were waiting for."

He punched a button. "Put him through, Maybelle." He lifted the handset. None of those cell phones for his important calls. Besides, the old desk phone was hardwired to a recording system in the false drawer, and he didn't want to fuss with changing that. Signals that float through the air felt too vulnerable. Technology had its uses where security was concerned, but he was more comfortable with an old fashioned hand set. He wanted his calls to speed along a landline without worrying about some hacker snatching his words out of the ether.

The voice on the other end of the line asked, "Does she suspect anything?"

"Not a thing. She's too busy mentally decorating her vice president's office."

"Is that what it took? I thought—"

"Just a ploy. Everything is fine."

"She may never forgive us for this, you know."

Pembroke chuckled. "She'll forgive us eventually. Don't worry. Everything is going according to plan."

Chapter Five

Thursday, April 7

AXEL PARKED HIS EXPEDITION under the Cattleman's portico and gave a mock salute to the bellboy, who was unloading luggage from a limo. "Good morning, Cody. I'm just here to meet someone."

"No worries, Mr. Garrison. Smells like snow, don't it?"

Axel tilted his head back and sniffed. The temperature had dropped overnight, and the air smelled of damp pines and impending precipitation. "Yes, it does. The ski resorts will be happy."

He moved through the lobby, nodding and smiling at another bellboy. He enjoyed the fact that, in just a few months, he'd come to know several people well enough to feel welcome, if not completely at home, in Eagle's Toe. Oddly enough, the place he felt most at home was on his eighty acres, purchased from Lucy Baxter, owner of the Lazy B. She was always glad to see him, and her cooks often spoiled him with fresh-baked cookies. He was well aware that his land purchase had made her solvent again. And he admired her pluck, turning her ranch into a resort for paying guests in order to keep it going.

It was only after the purchase was final that he learned that Thor and Rudy had hoped to buy the same land, as it bordered on the acreage they'd already accumulated. Thor's luxury cabin was on the northwest edge of that parcel. Axel's land was on the south edge. But it wasn't Axel's fault that they'd never let him in on their plans. When he arrived in Eagle's Toe, his cousins had assumed he'd soon be returning to New York. After all, he was raised on the East Coast. He must be a city boy.

In reality, Axel was raised on a large country estate three hours from Manhattan. Even the private prep school he'd attended was in the little village of Pawling, an hour's drive from the city. His father was the one who loved the urban life. Lester left Texas to go to college and never looked back. His brother Rudy, and Rudy's family, had stayed in Texas, at least until Thor left for Colorado.

Axel stopped at the free coffee bar in the lobby to pour himself a cup. He stirred sugar into his brew and helped himself to an apple fritter, closing his eyes with pleasure at the first sweet bite. As he sipped his coffee, it occurred to him that Rudy hadn't actually stayed in Texas either. He'd spent his life working all over the world. He just wanted his family rooted in Texas so he could claim that he'd remained a Texan while scolding his brother Lester for living life elsewhere.

That realization made Axel smile. No wonder his cousins suspected some sneaky motive behind him buying the land they wanted. Antagonism appeared to be a family tradition. That explained why Axel and his father were often at odds with each other. On top of that, while Lester loved the excitement of New York City and the stock market, Axel dreamed of acquiring a different kind of stock. Livestock. In fact, he'd already begun. He wondered what his cousins would say about that.

His call to Dustin had been a waste of time. His younger brother sounded irritated that his work day had been interrupted for so trivial a matter as their father's health. The whole exchange had left a bad taste in Axel's mouth. Someday, he'd have to have a long talk with Dustin about family. On the other hand, Dustin was the sibling who had turned out the most like their father. So what was the point?

He finished his coffee and fritter, then tossed the cup and napkin into a trash container. He glanced around as the time approached for him to meet Taylor. He didn't see any likely suspects. The few men moving through the lobby did not linger as if waiting for anyone. He spotted the blue-haired spitfire he'd collided with the day before and snorted softly. She was pacing along the wall near the entrance to the Il Vaccaro restaurant, studying the historical photos hanging there, pictures of Eagle's Toe from the 1860s to the present day. Axel let his eyes linger on her perfect figure. Her tailored pantsuit and stacked heels were meant for a day in the office. She carried a computer bag over one shoulder. He tilted his head to one side. If she wore Armani, she more likely owned the company than worked for it. He averted his eyes quickly when she glanced casually around. He pretended he hadn't seen her and walked over to the young woman behind the registration desk.

"Excuse me." He paused to read her name tag. "Janice?" He smiled, and she smiled back. "I'm supposed to meet someone here this morning. Have you seen him? His name is Taylor."

Janice looked amused. "Your 'he' is a 'she' and she's right over there. The lady with the blue hair."

Axel felt dismay land on him with both feet. He managed to mutter, "Thank you." Then he arranged his features before turning in Taylor's direction. It occurred to him that his father never specified Taylor's gender in their phone call. A tiny part of his mind wondered if that was done on purpose. Leave it to Lester to make his life more awkward. Oh, well. When she found out he was the person she was there to meet, she'd probably walk away. If she wore Armani, she didn't really need this job, that was for sure. He wondered what his father was paying her.

He forced a smile and approached her with his hand extended. "Taylor? I'm Axel Garrison."

Her dismay mirrored his own. "You've got to be kidding me." She crossed her arms and ignored his offered hand.

Axel dropped his arm. "I see we are equally delighted to make each other's acquaintance. How about this? I will buy you a replacement blouse, and we can start fresh."

She examined him critically from thick, dark hair to barn jacket, faded jeans, and mud-caked hiking boots, and he tingled all over, as if her blue eyes were shooting tiny icicles. Her voice made her opinion of his wardrobe crystal clear. "No offense, but I will pick out my own blouse. You may, however, pay for it. Lucky for you, I got it on sale. Eight hundred and fifty dollars."

Axel pulled out his wallet and counted out the cash. "Nice to know you're a thrifty shopper," he said, with the slightest hint of sarcasm.

He was surprised when she didn't end the arrangement right then. Instead, she accepted the cash as if it were a ten dollar bill, slipped it into her computer bag, and asked, "Shall we get started? I understand I'm assisting you with your father's biography."

Axel concealed his surprise with a wave toward the front entrance. "Great. We'll be working at my place. It's a ways out of town, so I thought I'd pick you up and bring you back later."

"I have a rental car," she said briskly. "I will follow you to your place."

Axel hesitated. "Four-wheel drive?"

She looked exasperated. "How do I know? It's a car. A sedan. Shiny and new."

Axel rubbed a hand over his jaw. "Gee, I wouldn't advise taking a rental car to my place."

"And why not?" Her attitude verged on flippant, moving quickly to snippy. "I am capable of driving a car."

Axel shrugged. She'd find out soon enough. "If that's the way you want it, okay. I'm parked out front in the black Expedition. I'll wait for you to pull around and you can follow me to my place."

"Good. Fine. I'll go get my car, since Yokelville doesn't understand the concept of valet parking." She turned on her heel and stomped off.

Axel felt a grin creeping up on him. He knew he shouldn't let her take a shiny new rental car up to his cabin, but she was obviously furious at the fact that her new employer was the jerk who'd messed up her blouse. There was no way she'd listen to him anyway. Maybe after today, she'd lend him more credence. Meanwhile, he figured he'd better make a phone call while he waited in the Expedition. He had a feeling they would both be glad he did.

Chapter Six

TAYLOR STOMPED ACROSS THE PARKING LOT. She couldn't believe her miserable luck. How could her father send her out here to spend time with such an oaf? She felt this might be the last straw. Even worse, he was movie-star handsome. If only he weren't dressed like a ranch hand. Then again, how many ranch hands carried hundred-dollar bills around in their wallets?

She warmed at the memory of his gaze focused on her soaked chest but snapped herself out of that in a hurry. She didn't have time for physical attraction. She had her eyes on a New York City prize, and she would not be dissuaded by her body's traitorous yearning every time Axel came within three feet of her.

She let her mind wander to the glorious mahogany office furniture she'd found on the web the night before. And the art work she wanted on the walls. Surely Daddy would spring for a Van Gogh. She calmed herself as she got into the rental car.

"Keep your eyes on the prize, Taylor," she said firmly. "Eyes on the prize."

The car started up and she maneuvered it through the lot and around the hotel to the portico. There he was in his black Expedition, leaning out of his window to look at her, waving and grinning like a fool. Well, okay, beaming at her like some movie star acknowledging adoring fans. She forced a smile and wiggled her fingers at him.

She had to admit, she would consider him drop dead gorgeous, if he wasn't such a buffoon. At least she'd have someone decent to look at while she was pretending to be his underling. Thank goodness she'd been a procrastinator in school. It forced her to type all her own papers, and that meant she was pretty good with a keyboard. Not like her roommate, Miss Early For Everything, who would handwrite her assignments ahead of time and have her father's secretary type them up for her. Now, Taylor realized her typing skills were going to win her a vice presidency. And with that kind of allowance—income, she corrected herself—spending time with Jackson would be her top priority.

As she followed the mud-encrusted Expedition onto Highway 50 and west, she felt a teensy twinge of responsibility. She should probably plan on being present in exchange for her salary. Maybe for the first year or so, she would hunker down and learn what she needed to know to run the company. Get in good with Daddy. Otherwise, her competitive siblings might try to edge her out. Especially if they got wind of how she earned her position.

"Slow down, idiot," she muttered as the Expedition sped up to seventy. "The fool doesn't even know how to drive when someone is following him." But traffic wasn't bad. In fact, she'd been astonished at how light the traffic was from the moment she got in the rental car. Colorado was not New York.

A large truck drove by in the other direction, pulling a horse trailer. That comforted her. Horses had been her passion since childhood, and Jackson allowed her to satisfy that desire. All in good time, she thought. First, get the salary. She didn't want to be like some of her schoolmates, waiting for the day when she would inherit. And she didn't want to have to ask for an allowance every month. She wanted to be independent, but she wasn't stupid enough to walk away from her father's wealth. She would have to juggle her personal goals with those of her father. Strike a balance.

Lost in thought, she had to brake hard to follow Axel when he took an off-ramp she wasn't expecting. At the bottom, they turned south on a narrow two-lane road. Clumps of snow still littered the landscape, and there was a definite nip to the air. Ten minutes later, the Expedition pulled off the road onto a dirt driveway. Five minutes after that, Taylor realized it wasn't a driveway. It was a dirt road. He passed a grouping of mailboxes, and when the dirt road began to wend even higher, Taylor gripped her steering wheel. She felt the bottom of the car scrape a high spot. That unnerved her. The road was now only wide enough for one vehicle at a time. Jaw clenched, Taylor noticed that the patches of snow were lying closer to the road, and the snowmelt had made the road extremely muddy. Up ahead, the Expedition moved farther and farther away, its huge tires flinging chunks of dark mud behind.

Now she was really worried. She could feel the little rental car slipping and sliding on the mud. She tried to speed up to catch the Expedition, but her tires didn't have enough grip for this terrain. Her jaw clenched tightly as every tap on the accelerator brought another queasy slide. The trees were thinning out, and the road was even muckier, as the sun melted more snow. She realized the Expedition was out of sight, and a flicker of fear made her push the accelerator again. This time, the wheels spun madly, and the car twisted to the left. She turned the wheel to the right, hoping to get some grip, but when it came, she wasn't expecting it, and the car jolted forward and tipped nose-down into a two-foot ditch.

The airbag did not deploy, so she knew she hadn't landed hard, but it shook her up. Her hands trembled, and when she tried to open the door, it jammed against a hillock of mud.

Taylor beat her hands on the steering wheel and screeched, "I hate you, I hate you, I hate you!"

As if hearing her rant, the Expedition reappeared, moving slowly down the hill toward her on its oh-so-smug tires.

As Axel's vehicle approached, a spark of revenge inspired Taylor to close and lock her door, then slump in her seat, letting the seat belt hold her weight. She heard his car door shut as he got out to check on her. She bit her lip to keep from laughing. She heard him try her door.

"Are you all right?" He sounded concerned.

She didn't move. His voice grew more intense. "Taylor?!" He knocked on the window. "Wake up!" He banged on the roof of the rental. She wondered how far he would go. Would he try to break in? There were plenty of rocks about. Or did he have one of those window-breaking devices in his SUV? Maybe she'd taken her charade far enough.

She sat up and pretended to be woozy. When she saw the look of alarm on Axel's face, she felt a pang of guilt. She tried to open her door again, but it would only move an inch. The engine was still running, so she opened her window instead. "Why on Earth did you let me drive this car up this road?" Her guilt disappeared as anger flooded back in.

Axel's shoulders relaxed. "You may recall that my plan was to drive you up here and bring you back."

"You might have explained about the mud," she snapped.

Axel crossed his arms over his chest. "You made it obvious you didn't want to hear anything I had to say."

"Oh, so now it's my fault?"

Axel turned sideways and stared off into the distance. "You should be a little more polite if you want help getting out of that car."

"I don't need your help." Taylor's anger had turned to cold, calm fury. She unfastened her seat belt, pulled her computer bag and purse off the floor, and shimmied halfway out the window. Realizing she needed to go feet first, she retreated, rearranged, and managed to get one leg over the door. How did those race car drivers do it? She grabbed hold of the top of the door frame and maneuvered her other leg through the window. Inch by inch, she scooted her bottom over the edge until her legs dangled. With one last effort, she was out.

And her beautiful new shoes were ruined as her feet sank two inches into the mud. She tried to move, lost her balance, and fell back against the car.

Axel applauded. "That was amazing. Are you a gymnast or something?"

Taylor glared at him. "A gentleman would offer a hand."

He gaped. "You just insisted you didn't need my help." He turned to look down the road again.

Taylor closed her eyes for a moment to calm herself down. Then, "Why are you staring into the distance?"

Axel pointed. "I was looking for that tow truck." A big red-and-white truck was lumbering up the muddy road.

"That was fast. How did he get here so soon?" Then it dawned on her, and she was livid. "You knew this was going to happen! You arranged for all of this!"

Axel patted the air with both hands as he backed away. "Now, now. That's not true. I didn't know you would slide off the road. I just figured your little rental car might get stuck in the mud. I told Brady at the garage that I'd pay for his tow truck to make the trip, even if you didn't get stuck."

Taylor used both hands to free her right foot from the mud so she could take a step forward. Then she freed the left. Each step landed squishily in more mud. She ground her teeth. When she reached him, she would scratch his eyes out. Or at least leave something for him to remember her by.

Axel waved at the tow truck. He glanced back to see how Taylor was doing just as she lost her balance. He rushed to help her, but rushing was not wise in the slimy mud. One foot slid grandly toward her, accidentally hitting her ankle as he went down on his backside.

Taylor saw him coming and could not get out of the way. She waved her arms in the air, struggling for balance, but when his foot made contact, she pitched forward and sprawled on top of him. Her computer bag plopped a few feet away, splattering them both with mud.

Once again, Axel look worried. "Did I hurt you? Are you all right?"

Taylor braced her hands against his biceps, searching for leverage. Their size and strength gave her pause. She was pressed against his abdomen, which rippled beneath her. The man was a hunk! A shiver of desire raced through her. She found herself looking into his eyes. He met her gaze, and for a millisecond, she thought he returned that desire.

Then she noticed that a glop of mud had landed on the tip of his nose, and she burst out laughing. When he crossed his eyes, trying to focus on the mud, she laughed harder. A moment later, he was laughing, too. Soon they were both gasping for air, overcome by the hilarity of the situation. Pausing to breathe, Taylor realized that her lips were mere inches from Axel's. He seemed to notice at the same moment. They froze.

Brady's voice startled them both. "Mud wrestling, eh? That's one way to pass the time while you wait for a tow."

Chapter Seven

WITH BRADY'S HELP, AXEL AND Taylor managed to get to their feet. The two men then assisted Taylor, whose shoes had become one with the mud. Axel opened the tailgate of his Expedition and boosted Taylor onto it.

"I'm really sorry," he said. "I didn't mean for you to get all muddy. I was trying to reach you before you fell. I sure didn't mean to kick you."

Taylor gave him a grim smile. "I know. It's okay. I deserved it. When you came up to my car window, I was faking. I wasn't really knocked out."

"Even Steven? We can start over?"

"Even Steven," said Taylor. She sighed as she surveyed the mud that covered her. "I think I should go back to the hotel and get cleaned up. Would you retrieve my computer and my purse?"

"Sure. You wait here. I'm going to help Brady load the rental car onto the truck." He fetched her things, then assisted Brady.

As the rental car was being hoisted onto the truck bed, Brady said, "Why is her hair blue?"

Axel grinned. "Fashion. She's from New York."

"That's where you're from, right?"

"Correct. And that's why I know about blue hair. Say, would you mind giving her a lift back to the the Cattleman's? She needs to get cleaned up, and so do I. I'm afraid if I wait until after I drive her back down, I'll have dried mud in places I shouldn't."

"No problem. I'll throw a blanket over my front seat. Glad to do it." He lifted a brow. "She's a real cutie. You're lucky I'm a married man."

Axel shrugged but had to smile. "Yes, and she's even more attractive without the mud. But she doesn't like me very much. Especially after this morning."

Brady gave him a knowing look. "Oh, she likes you all right. She just doesn't know it yet."

Axel grinned and shook his head. "I'm not so sure about that. Thanks a lot, Brady. I'll go tell her she can hitch a ride back to the hotel with you."

Taylor had found a towel in the back of the SUV and was wiping mud off her feet. She'd already done the best she could with her face. "I hope you don't mind," she said, holding up the towel.

"Not at all. That's what it's there for. Say, we both need to clean up, so I asked Brady to give you a ride back to the hotel. If it's all right with you , we can start over tomorrow."

"Great idea. We can work in my suite, if you like. It would save you some gas."

"I have animals to tend to," said Axel, "so I prefer working at my place. But we'll play it by ear. How's that?" He extended a hand. To his relief, Taylor took it without hesitation. Then Axel had an idea. "If you walk to the tow truck, your feet will be covered with mud again. Let me help you." He swooped her up into his arms before she could refuse.

Taylor cried out in surprise, then wrapped her arms around Axel's neck. He grinned like an idiot all the way to the tow truck.

Chapter Eight

TAYLOR IGNORED THE STARES AS she walked through the lobby of the Cattleman's. The mud that covered her had begun to dry, and when she paused to wait for the elevator, she was mortified to see that she'd left a trail of mud on the marble floors. Her computer and her purse bounced against her hip, and every time they did, they knocked off more dried mud. She carried her ruined shoes in one hand. After she took them off to towel her feet, she couldn't get them back on again. Nor did she want to.

The elevator opened, and the couple inside looked startled at the sight of her.

"Mud wrestling," she said with a straight face. "It's all the rage."

They sidled out, and she had the elevator to herself, all the way up to her suite.

She tried to maintain her anger at Axel, but instead, she kept flashing back to the two of them on the ground and him with a Hershey's Kiss of mud on the end of his nose. Torsos pressed together. Those abs. Those biceps. Those shoulders. And the easy way he'd swooped her up into his arms. Those thoughts kept her warm as she disrobed and stood under the shower.

Once she got out, she put on a casual outfit—her favorite jeans, a lacy tee, and a pale blue zip-up fleece. She'd packed plenty of clothes, but she'd only brought three pairs of shoes. It never occurred to her that she'd be tromping through mud. She selected athletic socks and running shoes for the moment, and resolved to go out and look for some footwear more suitable to the terrain.

31

But first, she wanted to take a jab at her father. She spread her muddy garb on the bathroom floor, including the computer bag, and snapped a few pictures, which she immediately texted to Daddy's secretary. "Please show these to my father and tell him I want a Van Gogh for my office wall when I'm done."

Maybelle was a sweet lady who'd been her father's secretary for twenty years. She was used to getting Taylor's texts and passing them on, since her old-fashioned father claimed he didn't know how to do such things.

She was just about to leave the suite in search of a shoe store when she received a reply from Maybelle. "He asked if you're hurt?"

She texted back, "No. I'll call him later." She thought about telling them the car was totaled, but she'd do that on the phone. Too much drama in a text. Besides, Maybelle would worry. She tucked her phone away and headed out.

The morning sun was hiding, but even with low clouds threatening precipitation and everyone saying, "It smells like snow," Taylor enjoyed her exploration of the historic district of Eagle's Toe. The brick buildings, the old-fashioned signage, and the cleanliness of the place made her feel as though she were walking through a well-kept amusement park. The ice cream shop was doing a brisk business. The bookstore was full of people. Across the street, there was a line of people at the door of a little restaurant called the Itty Bitty. And the bakery on the corner was also packed with the early lunch crowd.

She kept walking east, toward the corner with the sign that read "Mina's Boutique." The girl behind the hotel registration desk had told her she would find everything she needed at Mina's.

Taylor was doubtful. But her quest today wasn't for quality. It was for expendable footwear that would keep her feet dry when she slogged through mud. She could hear classical music as she approached the entrance. Inside, she was surprised to see a woman at an old piano. The music was live, and the piano alcove was full of ladies at tables, lingering over coffee, tea, and pastries. The girls behind the registers were busily ringing up sales. Taylor stood for a few moments, inhaling the aroma of fresh coffee and looking for a sign that would direct her to a shoe department.

A cheerful middle-aged woman with a big smile and a twinkle in her eye greeted her. "Hello! Welcome to my boutique. I'm Mina. Can I help you find something? Or did you come for the music hour?"

Taylor couldn't help but smile back. The woman was wearing a long plaid skirt, black boots, and a lightweight blue sweater. It wasn't an outfit Taylor would have picked out, but it worked for the other woman. "I need some sturdy boots or hiking shoes. Something that won't fall apart in the mud."

"Oh, I've got just what you need. This way." Mina turned and led her toward a door at the far end of the shop. "We've just received our spring stock," she said, "and in Eagle's Toe, that means shoes for every kind of weather."

Taylor had expected the place to be stocked with inexpensive merchandise, but the quality of the clothes she passed was surprisingly good. "I hope you have my size. I have very small feet."

"I'm sure I've got something that will fit." Mina seemed certain she'd be able to meet Taylor's needs. Taylor followed her through the door and was surprised to find herself in an expansive shoe store.

"Your shop is a lot bigger than it looks from the outside."

"I've recently expanded," said Mina, as if that explained everything. "Here we are. Hiking boots and rubbers. You know, to wear over your dressy shoes?" She eyed Taylor's feet. "I'm guessing you wear a size five?"

"You have a practiced eye," said Taylor. She picked out three different styles. "I'll try these."

"Excellent. I'll be right back."

Taylor found a Victorian love seat and perched on the edge of it. She'd expected plastic benches and ugly racks holding cheap products. Instead, the room itself was a delight, richly decorated with period furniture, including the shoe racks. Before she had time to take it all in, Mina was back, carrying six boxes in her arms.

"I brought a few extras, just in case," she said cheerfully. She pulled up a bench with a slanted ruler on the front, the only piece of furniture that belonged in a shoe store. "May I help you get these on?"

Taylor settled back on the love seat and allowed herself to be pampered. Mina was a talker, and she had a nonstop patter going as she gently shoe-horned a pair of hiking boots onto Taylor's feet.

"You're new in town. Will you be staying long?"

"I'm not sure. These feel a bit loose."

"That's because you'd be wearing thicker socks, but we can try this other style if you'd rather." She opened a second box. "I heard you were working for Axel Garrison."

Taylor was surprised. "Where on Earth did you hear that?"

"Small town," said Mina. "And my cousin is married to the owner of the Cattleman's. We talk every day."

"Oh, I see." Taylor hated the idea of working for Axel. She chose her words carefully. "Actually, I'm here to collaborate with him on a project."

"He's fallen in love with Colorado," said Mina. "It's nice to have a Garrison in town who's interested in the rural way of life."

"There are other Garrisons in town?" Taylor asked innocently.

Mina nodded. "Thor Security across the street? That's Thor Garrison. And Thor's brother, Ulysses, does fundraising for the hospital." She leaned back and eyed the hiking boots on Taylor's feet. "Those look perfect. Do you want to walk around in them?"

Taylor did so. They were comfortable and warm. "Will they fend off the mud?"

Mina's eyes widened. "Oh, you must be working up at his cabin. Springtime is mud season." She grinned. "These are treated with a water-repellent chemical, and they do a good job of shedding mud and moisture. But you may want to include a pair of these overshoes. You can pull them on over your normal shoes, or wear them alone and change into your shoes when you get where you're going."

Mina pulled rubbers out of a box and eye-balled them to see if they would work for Taylor. She continued to babble as she handled the shoes. "Thor is trying to get the town to approve a luxury housing development. And in addition to him pestering the city council, there's all the buzz going around among the ranchers about oil and gas and freaking," she said.

Taylor hid her smile. "You mean fracking?"

Mina laughed. "Yes, that's it. Horrible stuff. Some new people came into town and wanted to talk to the town council about how much money everyone would be making. They told us that modern oil wells can be unobtrusive. That was their word. Well, we may be rural, but we have TV like everyone else. We know what's going on. The council turned them down flat."

"Good for them," said Taylor, slipping her foot into one of the rubber boots.

"Of course, there's always a couple with a greedy gleam in their eye, you know. But they were outvoted." She pulled out a different pair of boots. "Sad thing is, there's a few families around that are barely making it. The Pattersons and the Shanes might benefit from the offers, but from what I've read about that stuff, the whole community would suffer." She shook her head. "Glad I don't have to make those big decisions." She sat back and admired the rubber boots on Taylor's tiny feet. "What do you think? I believe you may need both."

Taylor took Mina's advice and selected overshoes along with the hiking boots. "So Axel's cousins aren't interested in the rural life?"

Mina looked surprised. "Did I say that? Well, to tell the truth, they love it here, but they keep trying to turn it into something it's not. Thor and his father are planning to build luxury homes on the land they've already acquired, and they've been working with the town council to get zoning changes and all those details taken care of so they can start building." Mina rang up Taylor's purchases as she chatted. "As long as they were just talking about what they wanted to do, everyone sort of let it slide off. Pipe dreams. That sort of thing. But when they began asking for zoning changes? Well, there have been a number of heated exchanges at the town council meetings. Not everyone thinks it's a good idea."

Taylor handed Mina her charge card. "And Axel moved here to reinforce their efforts?"

"Oh, no. On the contrary. He bought eighty acres from the Lazy B Ranch, and the first thing he did was have the old barn rebuilt. Then he took on some of the reindeer the Lazy B had brought in as an experiment. And when Sunny Finch—she's married to Brady Felton over at the Garage—when Sunny rescued some neglected alpacas, Axel offered to take care of them, since she doesn't have much space for grazing animals." She handed Taylor a pen and a charge slip to sign. "Poor Axel. His cousin Thor was furious because he and his father wanted to buy that land. They were holding off until the Lazy B lowered the price, but Axel jumped in and paid what Lucy was asking. Lucy Baxter owns the Lazy B."

Taylor's mind was reeling from information overload. She signed the charge slip. "Whose side are you on?" she asked. "Axel's or Thor's?"

Mina hemmed and hawed, then confessed in a whisper, "Let's just say Axel kept Lucy from losing her ranch, so most of us around here are pleased as punch to have him move in. Not that we don't love all the Garrisons. Lovely people. Especially Thor's wife, Ashley. She and I own a gallery together. But Axel? It's as if he should have been born here." She walked Taylor back through the front of the boutique. "If you need anything else, just let me know." She handed Taylor a business card before turning away to tend to another customer.

Taylor strolled along the street. She picked up a local paper in the bookstore. Then she crossed to The Muffin Man bakery and treated herself to cookies. The woman behind the counter wore a name tag that said "Karen" and she had friendly eyes and a smile as warm as fresh bread. Taylor chatted with her for a few minutes and ended up buying twice as many cookies as she'd intended.

Out of curiosity, she ambled east again, past the Itty Bitty restaurant. She paused in front of the art gallery next door—she was sure it must be the one that Mina co-owned—before moving on to peer through the plate glass window of Thor Security. A large Doberman pinscher lunged at the window, barking loudly. A handsome blond Adonis commanded, "Quiet, Rocky!" and the dog fell silent and returned to a bed in the corner. The man glanced at her and waved, then turned back to his conversation with a customer. Taylor realized he must be Thor Garrison.

Axel was much better looking than his cousin, but she reminded herself that it didn't matter. After all, she was here to do her father a favor and earn a vice presidency and a fat paycheck, not moon over Axel Garrison.

She decided it was time to head back to the Cattleman's. She wanted to type up some notes on the information she'd gathered from Mina before she forgot the details. This whole small town thing might work to her advantage. Any and all information would be welcome. Anything to get her out of here and back to Manhattan.

Back in her suite, she settled on her favorite sofa and selected a cookie from the bakery sack. She unfolded the town paper and gaped at the headline.

"Garrisons at War Over Zoning Changes."

Chapter Nine

Friday, April 8

AXEL RUSHED THROUGH HIS MORNING chores so he could head into Eagle's Toe and fetch Taylor. He had a feeling their working relationship was doomed. She was too prissy for outdoor living, and she was way too absorbed in her wardrobe. He had to admit that she was cute as a button, trying to walk in the mud in her expensive heels. And the jolt of electricity that coursed through him when he picked her up and carried her to the tow truck was real enough. That energy was still singing through his veins. Oh, yes, she was easy on the eyes, all right. He couldn't wait to chew his father out over this development. What was Lester thinking? He wanted this biography written in half the time it should take—no, strike that, a third of the time it should take—and then he sent a so-called assistant who was so gorgeous, it made thinking about the project nearly impossible.

On top of that, Axel had stayed up until two a.m. working on his novel. Biography or no biography, he needed to finish his book if he was going to have a chance of making it as a writer. He couldn't just let it languish. He would have to work on both projects simultaneously. That's all there was to it.

He managed to make it to the Cattleman's by eight-thirty. Taylor was waiting for him. She was much more sensibly dressed, wearing jeans and mud boots and a blue hoodie that matched her hair color. Well, they were designer jeans, but all in all, she looked ready for a work session at the cabin, and she might even be able to walk through the spring mud to get from the SUV to the front door.

"Good morning." Taylor was all business. She laid the local newspaper on the seat between them. "It looks like your cousins are gearing up for a big argument over the local zoning laws. There's a line in there somewhere about how you threw a wrench into their development plans by buying the Baxter acreage."

Axel glanced at the paper. "Are you planning to keep a scrapbook of my activities?"

Taylor tilted her head to one side. "If it will help us write this biography, I'm willing to try anything. The sooner we finish, the better."

Axel snorted. He'd been so busy fantasizing about how cute she was, he'd forgotten how annoying she could be. "Buckle up. Have you had breakfast? I picked up coffees and donuts at The Muffin Man."

Taylor inhaled gratefully. "Are you already trying for Employer of the Year?" She pried the lid off a styrofoam cup and sipped at the contents. "Mmmm. Perfect temperature. Any maple bars?" She opened the white pastry bag and selected a sleek, heavily frosted maple bar.

Axel grinned. Maybe she was just grumpy because she hadn't had her coffee yet. Traffic was light at this hour, and after his late night pounding the keys, he was just as glad. "Do you mind handing me one of those?"

Taylor wrapped the bottom half of a donut in a napkin and handed it over.

"Thanks," said Axel. "So how shall we start? Have you got a plan?"

"Once we get to the cabin, I can set up my laptop and we can go from there. I spent time online last night researching a few biographies of famous figures. And frankly, I wasn't too impressed. They were like reading history books."

"I seriously doubt that's what my father has in mind. He told me he wants this to be a gift for the family. Everyone will get a bound volume. And he wants a lot of information in there about my mother, too."

"What's her name?"

"Marla. She died almost two years ago." The painful memory snuck up and stabbed him in the heart, even after all this time.

"Oh, I'm sorry." Taylor frowned. "I thought I heard someone say your father is married. Second wife?"

Axel grunted, not a pleasant sound. "Bambi. Can you believe that? Who names their kid Bambi?"

"A Disney fan?" Taylor sipped coffee. "I take it you don't approve."

Axel took a deep breath and let it out. "My father's a grown man. He can do what he wants. Never mind that all his kids think she's a money-grubbing gold digger. She hasn't stopped writing checks since the day they got married."

Taylor perked up. Maybe this would lead to some dirt on Lester. "You think he's letting her spend your inheritance?"

Axel shook his head. "I don't care about that. My mother's family had money, too. She made sure everything she brought into the marriage was divided amongst us kids. She told me once she never wanted us to do without. She said she'd done enough of that for all of us combined when she was a little girl."

Taylor licked icing off the last third of her maple bar. "She sounds like a very practical woman. May I ask how she died?"

"Plane crash."

"Oh no." Sympathy flowed with the words. "I'm so sorry. Was it one of those awful tragedies in Malaysia?"

"No. Small plane. She was involved in a lot of businesses on her side of the family, mostly located in Florida and Georgia. Big manufacturing plants, set out in the suburbs. She was very hands-on. And she had a plane and a pilot. When she went to board meetings, she flew." He shuddered. "To this day, I can't get on a four-seater. Not even on the ground. The pilot was killed instantly, but Mom...she survived the crash, for a while. At least I got to spend her last few weeks with her." He felt his eyes sting with the buildup of tears and wiped them away furtively. "It was rough. When people ask, we just say she died in the crash. The rest is too painful to relive."

"That's so awful," said Taylor.

"Are you close to your mother?"

Taylor shrugged. "I suppose I was when I was little. But I was mostly a Daddy's Girl. By the time I went away to college, it was like my mother and I came from different planets. Even now, she looks at me sometimes and gets this expression on her face like she's wondering, 'Who took over my daughter's body?' She's the perfect CEO's wife. She handles all of my father's entertaining. She goes with him whenever he needs her, and she's Daddy's representative at charity events."

"Is she happy?"

Taylor shrugged. "I guess so. She's still married to my father. That means she's happy, right?"

Axel's brows rose. "You never know. People stay together for lots of reasons."

"Was your mother happy?"

Axel's chin trembled for a moment. He cleared his throat. "I think she was. During those last few weeks, we talked a lot when she was lucid. Sometimes she didn't know what had happened or where she was. Sometimes she thought I was a little boy, and every now and then, she thought I was her high school sweetheart. But mostly she was coherent. When she was conscious. I kept my computer nearby and when she'd ask me to tell my siblings things, I'd write them down so I wouldn't forget."

"Gee, that must be powerful stuff."

Axel felt guilty. "It was. It is." He glanced at her sideways. "I haven't had the nerve to go back and read it in a long time."

"So you haven't shared it with your family?"

"No." And there were lots of parts he would take with him to the grave. He just couldn't bring himself to erase the files.

Taylor gazed out the window as the SUV labored up the hill toward the cabin. "Those files may come in handy before we're through with this biography," she said.

"We'll see," said Axel, even though he'd already decided there wasn't a snowball's chance in hell of him including those conversations with his mother.

Taylor tapped on the side window. "I thought you only had reindeer and alpacas. Where did the horses come from?"

Axel leaned forward to peer beyond her toward the barn, where a dozen horses milled about, pulling hay free from a bale beneath the hay shed. "Oh no," he groaned. "There must be a hole in the Lazy B's fence!"

Chapter Ten

AXEL WAS OUT OF THE VEHICLE as fast as he could go. "I've got to make sure they didn't get into the grain and pig out," he said, trotting for the barn.

Taylor was right behind him. She counted twenty reindeer scattered about, pawing through the snow to find grass. A few were sheltering beneath some trees, nibbling on a crust of lichen. They were watching the horses as if they were curiosities sent over for their amusement.

The eight alpacas were a different story. They were in the corral, and they were not pleased. They bleated and complained, probably telling Axel that someone was eating their hay. That thought made Taylor smile. Then she remembered she wasn't supposed to be enjoying herself.

She followed Axel into the barn, and sure enough, two horses were feasting on a sack of grain they'd knocked over.

"Oh no," he said. "I'd better call Lucy and get some help over here. I hope these two don't get colic." He pulled out his phone and punched up Lucy's information.

While Axel fussed with his phone, Taylor examined the horses. One was a buckskin mare with a black mane and tail, the other a blue roan gelding. The mare moved away when she approached, but the gelding turned thoughtful eyes in her direction and tossed his head as if to say, "Hi, how's it going?"

Taylor glanced around. Axel had left the barn. She spotted a coil of soft rope and picked it up. She let her muscle memory imitate what she'd seen the grooms do a hundred times at her Central Park stable. A moment later, she gently laid one end of the rope over the gelding's neck, made a loop on the other end and slipped it over his nose.

"You are a sweetheart," she said softly. "Obviously someone's pet. Let's see if we can help Axel deal with your buddies out there." She led the gelding to a bale of hay and used it as a mounting block. A moment later, she was up, riding bareback. The gelding's ears were alert and his manner was relaxed. She leaned forward and touched his sides with her heels. He moved obediently beneath her. The skittish mare decided she didn't want to stay in the barn alone and loped past them out toward the reindeer. Once outside the barn, Taylor rode the roan over to an astonished-looking Axel.

"Ask her what the blue roan gelding is called," she said.

Axel repeated her question, and then relayed the response. "Thunder. His name is Thunder."

"Is she sending someone over to round up the others?"

"Yes," said Axel. "And she's coming herself." He spoke into the phone again, then ended the call. He leaned against the corral and looked up at her. "I'm impressed. Where did you find the halter?"

"I made it." Taylor tried not to sound too smug. After all, it was just a little emergency halter. "Don't you have any tack in that barn?"

Axel shrugged. "I do now, thanks to you."

"No, I mean real tack. Bridles, saddles, harnesses?"

"Lucy gave me some old harness for the reindeer, but so far, I'm just trying to learn how to keep them alive and healthy. I don't have a sleigh or anything. She's got that stuff over at the Lazy B. She helps the Cattleman's Christmas fundraising for local animals by giving reindeer-drawn sleigh rides to the kids."

While Axel talked, Taylor indulged herself, using her feet and legs to put Thunder through a few paces.

Axel shook his head. "You're not even pulling on the halter."

"No need," she said. "Someone has spent a lot of time with this big boy. Makes me homesick."

"I thought you hated the country. After yesterday's mud fiasco, I figured you for a total city girl."

"I am a city girl," said Taylor defensively. "But that doesn't mean I don't know horses. I ride in Central Park every chance I get." And she wished she was there right now, with Jackson. "Wait here. I'm going to persuade those two paints to come back and join the group."

Taylor thoroughly enjoyed herself, showing off her equestrian skills in front of Axel. When Lucy Baxter and two ranch hands showed up, driving a beat-up old gray pickup, Taylor was pleased by the expressions on their faces. It gave her a thrill to have someone appreciate her abilities on a horse. Goodness knew she'd never seen that look of approval on her father's face.

Axel introduced her to Lucy. "Taylor, this is Lucy Baxter, the lady who sold me the land."

Taylor slipped effortlessly off Thunder's back and led him over to Lucy. "Nice to meet you," she said. "I adore your horse."

Lucy's gray frizzled hair and the laugh lines around her eyes made her look pleasant even when faced with wandering equines. She shook Taylor's hand and took the offered lead rope. "It's not often we have city folk come out who actually know how to ride," said Lucy. "Maybe you can talk this fellow into adding a horse or two to his menagerie. It just feels wrong to have a beautiful new barn like his and not put horses in it."

Taylor nodded. "I couldn't agree more. I think I like you, Lucy."

"Feeling's mutual," said Lucy. "Jeff, get Thunder saddled up. I'll collect Ruby and we'll take this lot back home. Red, you follow us in the truck and repair that fence once we've gone through it."

With Lucy taking charge, things moved quickly. Soon, Taylor and Axel were waving goodbye as Jeff and Lucy herded the rest of the horses toward her property. Red followed along behind, driving the old truck at a snail's pace to keep from rushing the horses.

Axel turned to Taylor. "I hope you don't mind, but before we get started, I need to make sure the reindeer are all accounted for and settle the alpacas down a bit."

"The reindeer look nice," said Taylor, wishing she'd had more time with Thunder. "Do they like people?"

"I've got twenty here, and I'd say ten of them tolerate being handled. A couple are very friendly, almost like pets. The rest are just livestock. They're all caribou and could care less about people, unless we're delivering hay. But Lucy told me they'll make good breeding stock."

Taylor was beginning to feel more and more comfortable. It wasn't Central Park, but the barn and corral were new. "I think I like the reindeer," she said. She climbed up on the fence and perched on top of a post, turning sideways to examine the alpacas. "Are the alpacas friendly?" She reached out to pet one.

"They're a little upset right now," said Axel.

And just as he said that, the alpaca nearest Taylor spit all over her. She shrieked in disgust. "He just puked on me!"

Axel patted the air to calm her down. "It's just rumen. It smells like puke, but it'll wash off."

Taylor jumped down and stood staring at the green mess all over her blue hoodie. "What is it with you and my clothes?"

"I'm really sorry," said Axel, but he couldn't entirely hide the fact that he was laughing at the sight of her. "Look, just add it to my bill, okay? And maybe you should stick to horses and reindeer. Come on inside. You can get cleaned up. I'll bring your things in from the car."

Once inside the cabin, Taylor stripped off the hoodie and dropped it on the floor. She found a kitchen towel, wet the end, and tried to clean the rumen off her designer jeans. Most of it came off, and she was mollified to see that it hadn't soaked through her hoodie to her silk blouse. The rumen was so nasty, it made the rustic bare-bones cabin almost acceptable.

After a few minutes, Axel came in, set her computer and her purse on the only table in the cabin, and found a plastic trash bag to stuff the hoodie into. He disposed of it outside. "Seriously," he said, "make a list. I'm going to owe you a complete wardrobe at this rate."

Taylor busied herself with pulling her computer out of its case and turning it on. "You enjoyed that way too much," she said tartly.

"Actually, what I enjoyed the most," said Axel, sounding sincere, "was the sight of you on the back of that horse. Even Lucy was impressed." Axel opened a cupboard and pulled out coffee and filters for the pot.

"Don't try to sweet talk me," Taylor grumped, but inside, she was pleased. "I'm surprised your father wants you to write his biography. You two are nothing alike."

Axel set the coffee down with a bang. "How on Earth could you possibly know that?!"

Taylor froze. Her eyes darted from side to side, looking for an explanation. At last, she sputtered, "Well, he's supposed to be a famous businessman, right? And you're more like a farm boy." She spread her hands, hoping that would cover her gaffe. She couldn't remember how much she was supposed to know about Lester Garrison.

Axel relaxed. "Oh, right. He probably told you all about our disagreements when he hired you to be my assistant. Sorry. When it comes to my father, I'm super paranoid. Coffee?"

"Yes, please." Taylor's fingers shook as she opened her word processing program. Pembroke hadn't said anything about pretending that Lester Garrison had hired her. He'd made it sound like he was sending her out as a favor, not that she was being paid by Lester. She would be sure to chew him out later. He'd almost caused her to blow her cover, and that would mean no corner office, no cushy job, and no fat salary. And if he'd sent her all the way out here, to work under these conditions, he'd better be prepared to make good on his promises, or else!

Most of the rest of the day was devoted to setting up an outline for the biography. But Taylor's heart wasn't in it. Her introduction to Thunder made her long even more for Jackson's company. At one, she took a break and walked around outside the cabin just so she could make a private phone call and talk to Jackson.

Axel seemed cooperative enough as they worked, but Taylor felt that his attention was also elsewhere. His conversation rambled from his love for Colorado to his dream of being a writer and how that affected his relationship with his father. She took notes but knew his heart wasn't in the biography. All he wanted to do was go out and play cowboy. And frankly, she couldn't blame him for that. She enjoyed their time outdoors. She loved the reindeer. She wanted to see their harnesses and hear the bells ring, and she wanted to brush them out and touch their antlers. She didn't care much about the alpacas. They could stay in the corral for all she cared and never show their faces.

At the end of the day when Axel drove her back down the hill to the Cattleman's Inn, Taylor realized that once again she would be spending her evening trying to type up notes from memory, because once the outline was established, they'd taken their conversation outdoors and done very little hands-on work with her computer.

After a quick shower, she ordered room service. Her brain was still humming with the thrill of riding Thunder and inhaling alfalfa and fresh air.

Clean and warm in soft pink sweats, she settled on the big sofa to watch the sunset. Her mind wasn't ready to concentrate. Her father was expecting her to call later, but she wasn't sure how long she'd be awake after so many hours in the fresh air and sunshine. She decided she would call Daddy early and surprise him.

She picked up her phone. Eight o'clock in New York. She'd try his office first. His landline wasn't even digital. Daddy could be such a dinosaur.

A male voice picked up. "Hazen Industries. Donald Hazen, Vice President of Marketing speaking."

Taylor bristled. Vice President of Marketing?! Was her father handing out titles to everyone? "Don? Why are you in the City? What do you mean, vice president?"

"Oh. Er, hi Taylor. Um, Dad and I were just...talking over a few things."

Taylor's mood shifted from suspicion to anger. "Well, put him on the phone," she snapped. "I've got a few things to discuss with him myself!"

Chapter Eleven

AXEL DID HIS EVENING CHORES, doing a headcount of his livestock as he spread hay and filled feeders. This was usually the best part of his day, but this evening, he was consumed by thoughts of Taylor. She'd ridden Thunder like a natural. No, more than that. Like a girl with years of horseback riding behind her. And the memory of her thighs and pert behind becoming one with that horse would not leave him alone. Where had his father found her?

Maybe she was the daughter of a friend of his mother's. If that were so, it would explain why she seemed to know what his father was like. There'd been a lot of young women around their upstate farm, and he had dated a few of them, but he was sure if one of them had been Taylor, he would have remembered her. Every time he got near her, he could feel bolts of electricity flying back and forth between them. They made his skin tingle. How on Earth was he supposed to write a book about his parents with Taylor around? And what kind of help was she going to be when her very presence made concentration impossible?

He filled the water tubs and mucked out the barn before finally patting his favorite reindeer on the rump and heading into the cabin. After thinking about it, he decided there was no way that Taylor had met his parents while his mother was still alive. But if his father had hired her to work on the biography, they must have met, right? He wouldn't just send someone he'd never even interviewed, would he? Axel's imagination ran wild. But if Taylor had interviewed with Lester for this job, then why had she tried to cover up that she knew him?

Axel's head pounded as he put the kettle on to make instant coffee. He wanted to work on his novel tonight, but how would he make any progress if he couldn't stop thinking about Taylor? And he needed to figure out her relationship to his father.

Then it hit him.

Lester Garrison had made that stupid wedding toast at the Forbes reception, promising that Axel would be the next to marry. Now it all made sense. His father had sent Taylor to Colorado to seduce him! He probably didn't give a darn about his biography. It was all a sham. His father was trying to set him up with a woman who could tempt him into getting married, just like the old man had promised in front of God and everybody. And Axel wouldn't be a bit surprised if his father had placed a few bets with his friends about the whole affair.

The kettle whistled with fury, a sound that matched his mood perfectly. A biography, huh? The old man wanted a biography? What a joke. He just wanted to make sure that Taylor was around all day, every day, worming her way into Axel's heart, making sure he failed at his attempt to be a novelist. Well, he'd show her, and he'd get back at his father, as well. He'd just make stuff up. He'd give her so much information, she'd be typing half the night to get it all down on paper. Because during the day, he'd make her follow him around, doing chores and whatever else he could come up with. She'd have to record him or take notes, because he'd make it impossible for her to sit at her laptop.

Yes, that was the ticket.

And meanwhile, he'd save all his creative energy for his own book. He set his mug of coffee on the table and rummaged through his cupboards. He should have picked up takeout when he dropped Taylor off in town. Two cans of soup, a box of saltines, and a jar of creamy peanut butter was the total extent of his larder. He sighed, exasperated. Maybe he could tell Taylor to buy him some groceries.

He laughed out loud at the thought. Sure, let her run some errands for him while she was in town. That would keep her busy. Because if he was going to avoid fulfilling his father's fantasy about a wedding for Axel, he'd better do something to derail the friendship that was growing between himself and Taylor.

He smeared peanut butter on a pair of saltines and wondered what his cousins would think of him, living like a hermit while his inheritance grew with wild abandon in his late mother's Swiss bank account. Meanwhile, they were planning more ways to invest in Eagle's Toe real estate. So close genetically, and yet so very different. Just like their fathers.

He opened his laptop and forced himself to re-read the last few pages he'd written. He stared hard at the screen, disgusted with his production. Two weeks ago, his prose was flowing and his plot—a soul-searching quest for meaning in a mercenary world—had consumed him. Two weeks ago he thought he might be writing the next great bestseller. But two weeks ago, he hadn't met Taylor.

And now, as he skimmed through his file, page after page, it all sounded flat and self-absorbed. He groaned and muttered, "Crap. It sounds like crap. And boring crap at that." He stuffed a peanut-butter-and-saltine sandwich in his mouth and washed it down with coffee. "Maybe…" he mused. "Maybe…maybe my hero needs a love interest." He grinned as his fingers flew over the keys.

"After all," he said to himself, "if it's crap, it can't get much worse. I might as well get a little revenge."

Chapter Twelve

TAYLOR WAS SO ANGRY, SHE was pacing back and forth. Not even the glorious sunset could comfort her.

"Daddy, you send me out here to play spy for you, and as soon as I'm gone, you turn around and give *my* vice presidency to Donald! How could you?"

"Now, now, don't get all bent out of shape. You'll get your reward for helping me on this job. I promise you'll be a vice president, just like I said you would. Just keep digging. What new information have you got for me?"

Taylor wondered if she should share anything. There were a few things she'd learned that she hadn't told her father yet because she hadn't had a chance to type up all her notes. But she felt betrayed. She knew there weren't that many vice presidencies available in the company, so basically, he was planning to give her a meaningless title just to keep her quiet.

If he actually followed through on his promise, that is.

She should have seen this coming. Every prime opportunity went to one of her brothers. She always got leftovers. Granted, considering her father's fortune, they were delightful and expensive leftovers. Even so, when Donald was in college, he was offered a new apprenticeship every summer, opportunities to build his experience to the point where he could step into a management position in San Francisco the week after he graduated.

Taylor, on the other hand, went to equestrian camp for six weeks every summer. Not that she had complained, but as she looked back, it became obvious that she was being entertained while her brothers were being trained. Now she knew why. Her father was planning to turn the company over to her brothers and leave her out in the cold.

Pembroke's voice interrupted her reverie. "Well? Have you learned anything useful or not?"

Taylor composed herself. "I learned that Axel and his siblings are very unhappy about Lester's second wife."

"Ah, hell, honey, I told you that much before you left New York. I need details I can use as leverage. So get busy. Lester has moved our next negotiation up. He wants to meet next Friday, a week from today. Dig me up some dirt, girl!"

Taylor's phone beeped. "Hang on, Dad. I have another call." She tapped the screen. "Hello?"

"Hi, it's Axel."

"You sound cheerful," she snapped.

"And you sound pissed. Something wrong?"

Taylor thought fast. "I broke a nail. And in this town, who knows how long I'll have to live with it." She reined in her hostility. She still needed to be able to wheedle information out of him. "Sorry. What can I do for you?"

"I was wondering if you'd mind picking up some groceries for the cabin. You know, just basic stuff."

Taylor resisted the urge to growl into the phone. What was it with men? Her father was using her for a spy. Now Axel was using her for a shopping cart. She tried to sound calm. "What do you need?"

"Let's see. It's easier to tell you what I have."

"Okay. What do you have?"

"Peanut butter, crackers, and two cans of soup. And coffee and tea. That's what I have."

Taylor held the phone out in front of her face and glared at it, as if it were Axel. "Fine," she said at last. "I'll pick up some supplies."

"Do you need a list?"

"No. Sorry. I'm on the other line. You'll have to trust me."

"Okay. Will do."

She cut him off and started to tell her father she was back on the line, but before she could say anything, she heard Donald's voice.

"—finds out what you've got planned, she's going to be pissed."

Taylor felt her blood pressure rising. She tapped her finger against the phone. Her father had no idea how cell phones worked, so he wouldn't know she'd been listening. "I'm back, Daddy." She poured sweetness into her voice. "I've been thinking, if you could give me an idea of what kind of dirt you need, I could work more efficiently. Do you want financial misdeeds? Or tax evasion? Or sexual escapades?"

"Good Lord, Taylor! I don't want you thinking about that kind of stuff. I don't care who he sleeps with. I want to know if he's bluffing me financially. Is he holding out because he needs more money? Or does he just want to watch me twist in the wind? But anything you get me could be useful." He paused. "On second thought, sexual misconduct might make a nice weapon. You get busy. The meeting is next Friday."

Taylor hung up and plopped down on the big sofa. "Next Friday. How am I going to find out anything juicy by then? Axel hasn't said a single rotten thing about his father." She pouted for a while. It felt good. She pushed her bottom lip out as far as it would go. Well, that ruined it. Now she just felt silly.

A soft knock on the door announced the arrival of room service. Taylor dropped her head back against the cushion and wondered if she had anything left inside to help her make it to the door. Now she was sure her father was going to betray her. Donald's big mouth had let that cat out of the bag.

A hesitant voice called out, "Room service."

She dragged herself off the sofa. The boy at the door was the same goofy fellow who'd piled all her luggage on his dolly when she'd arrived. He looked nervous and uncomfortable. He nodded curtly to her and rolled the cart into the room.

"Where would you like this, ma'am?"

Taylor had an idea. She smiled warmly. "Over by the sofa, please. I'd like to watch the rest of the sunset."

He gave her a wary look but did as she asked.

Taylor fetched her purse and withdrew several bills. "Say, I just wanted to apologize for being so snippy the other day. I'd had a long tiring trip, and I wasn't very nice. I hope you'll forgive me." She glanced at his name tag. "Cody. What a great name." She handed him a twenty-dollar bill.

Cody's eyes bulged. "Thank you, ma'am. That's very generous of you."

Taylor tilted her head coquettishly. "If you're interested in doubling that tip, you can do me a little favor."

"Sure." He beamed. "Who do you want me to kill?"

Taylor laughed like she'd never heard that line before. "Oh, you don't have to kill anyone. But you will need these." She held up three one-hundred dollar bills.

Chapter Thirteen

Saturday, April 9

THE NEXT MORNING, TAYLOR was waiting under the portico, ready for Axel to pick her up. She had her computer and purse on one arm. She was casually dressed because she knew they would be tromping around the barn, and she was eager to get some real work done. She didn't mind working on a Saturday. The sooner they got done, the better. She needed Axel to read through her notes and let her know if they were accurate. She felt she had very little that could be used against his father. She needed to come up with specific questions that would lead Axel into saying things that Pembroke could use against Lester. Not that she felt like doing her father's bidding after he gave her job to Don, but Daddy still ruled the purse strings and maybe he'd come through in the end. She saw Axel's vehicle approaching with a horse trailer attached to the back and wondered what craziness awaited her today. As he pulled up next to her under the portico, she turned to the sliding lobby doors and waved for Cody to come on out.

A moment later, he did so, pushing a luggage dolly piled with cardboard boxes filled with groceries and paper goods.

"Just load them in the back seat," she said.

Axel got out of the SUV and came around the front of it, hands on his hips. "What the heck is this?"

Taylor smiled sweetly. "You asked me to pick up some supplies. Loading will go faster if you help Cody." She opened the front passenger door and got in, settling her computer bag on the floor by her feet and her purse on the seat.

When Axel finally got back behind the wheel, he gave her a strange look. "Why do I doubt that you did all that shopping? Maybe it's the four bags of chips and the six bags of cookies."

"Well, I did have some help in that area," she said innocently. When he shook his head and frowned, she said, "Is something wrong?"

"I have to make a detour to the large animal vet. One of the reindeer has a bleeding hoof."

Taylor felt a pang of regret. The timing of her little gag had turned out to be awkward. Still, Axel had asked for supplies, so it wasn't her fault that he wasn't in the mood for an over-the-top response. Even so, she felt bad because it was one of the reindeer. If it'd been one of the alpacas she could've let it bleed to death. Then she felt a pang of guilt, because she knew deep in her heart that wasn't true.

She said grimly, "Okay, I'm ready. Let's go."

As Axel drove, he asked, "Are you okay?"

"I'm fine."

"You don't sound fine."

Taylor sighed heavily. "I got some disappointing news last night. Don't worry. I'll get over it. I'm here to do a job, and although I've had a lovely time playing with all the animals and seeing the barn—it's fantastic by the way—I ended up spending hours last night typing up notes from memory. Once we take care of the reindeer, you need to go over what I've got so far and fill in some blanks for me."

Axel nodded. "Sounds like a plan."

Taylor relaxed. "Good." At least he wasn't fighting her on this.

The hoof was abscessed, and the visit to the vet took over an hour. When they got to the cabin, Axel unloaded the reindeer and bedded her down in the stable. Taylor was still hauling boxes of supplies inside when he joined her. Then it was time to check on the rest of the animals. Taylor was tempted to call her father and tell him to send ranch hands or she'd never get enough working time in with Axel to finish her task. Then she nixed that plan. Daddy was the last person she wanted to talk to at the moment. She could still feel the hurt of having him stab her in the back.

She needed to direct her conversations with Axel in an aggressive way if she was going to dig up any dirt on Lester Garrison. She didn't want to be stuck in Eagle's Toe forever! Well, it was only another seven days, but it already felt like forever. And although the reindeer were delightful, she missed Jackson like crazy. Maybe she could borrow Thunder from the Lazy B. She needed a horse fix in a bad way.

Finally, they sat down together at the kitchen table at one o'clock to look at the document on Taylor's computer. She didn't have a printer with her, so they sat close together to examine the screen as Taylor scrolled through her notes. She couldn't help but notice that Axel was wearing a manly scent, and she wondered idly what it was. But if she asked that kind of a question, she couldn't justify that it had anything to do with information about his father. Then she had a brilliant idea.

"Axel, does your father wear the same aftershave as you?"

Axel pulled his head back a bit to look at her. His brows met in the middle, and he said, "I don't wear any aftershave."

Taylor felt a hot rush of embarrassment. Her cheeks glowed red and she stumbled over her words. "Oh, I'm sorry. I, um, I could've sworn I smelled…." She struggled to think of the name of an aftershave. "…that I smelled Axe." She smiled brightly. "You know? Axe, worn by Axel?"

"Sounds like a commercial to me," he teased. He sniffed the air. "And your scent today? No, let me guess. *Eau de Caribou?*"

"Very funny. Someone had to hold her and cuddle her while the vet was working on her hoof."

Axel grinned. "Well, it's way better than *Parfum de l'alpaca.*"

Taylor stuck her tongue out at him for a microsecond, then scrolled further down the page. "What about this section?" she asked. "Can you think of anything your father said or did during the period after your mother's funeral that was very upsetting to you or to your brothers and sisters?"

Axel squinted at the screen, but he didn't reply right away. At last, he said, "I can think of hundreds of things he did at the funeral and afterward that infuriated me, but I can't say that there was anything wrong with his behavior. I was so angry that my mother had died, I couldn't think straight. I've been working really hard at learning to cut my dad some slack. Having her go down in that plane nearly destroyed him. She'd wanted one for a long time, and although she didn't have a pilot's license herself, she loved the fact that she had a plane and a pilot at her disposal so she could get around quickly wherever she wanted to go. Dad bought her that plane. And he has never forgiven himself. And I'm ashamed to say, I haven't forgiven him either."

Taylor pressed her lips in a thin line. How was she going to get Axel to say anything bad about his father? The harder she tried, the nicer he sounded, and the nicer he sounded, the better she liked him. It was getting more and more difficult to maintain the hostility necessary to play her father's dirty tricks on him.

"I don't know, Axel. Maybe this was a mistake. Maybe I'm not the right person to help you write your father's biography. There just seems to be a lack of information about the man. Even the things I found on Google don't help. Sure, he's a hard-edged business man. But those things are all public record. We don't just want to produce a printout of your father's business dealings. We need to know some personal stuff. If this biography is for your family, then you need to put your thinking cap on and come up with some really egregiously bad stuff you felt your father has done, either to you or your mother or your siblings. Once we come up with those things, you can explain how they turned out, and why maybe they weren't so bad, or what you learned from those things. We can do all of that. But we can't do any of it until you actually tell me some dirt about your dad."

Axel frowned. "I don't think my dad wants his biography to be a laundry list of his mistakes in life."

Taylor thought fast. "Of course not," she replied. "I was just trying to think of a way to get your muse started. After all, you're the writer. I'm just here to help." She sighed heavily and closed her laptop. "But as your typist, it's very frustrating when we're supposed to be building a written document, and I can't lay it all out on the table and look at it."

For the first time that day, Axel seemed interested in what was going on. "Oh, I understand completely. I have to print my own stuff out every night. I need to look at it in order to edit and reorganize it. Okay here's what we're going to do. We'll stop at an office supply store and buy you a printer. There's one in the old part of town, just around the block from Mina's boutique. We'll pick up printer paper, cartridges, everything. That way, when you have time in the evening, you can print out your notes and we can each have a copy to work on. How does that sound?"

Truth be told, Taylor thought it sounded like a whole lot more work for her. And she was getting pretty darn tired of this job. However, it was the first time he had shown any real interest in making progress on the biography. So she agreed.

On the way into town, Axel grew chatty. He seemed to want to say something but wasn't sure how to say it. Or at least, that was the impression that Taylor got. He began, "You know, Taylor, I was really impressed with what you did with Thunder yesterday morning. You really know something about horses. And you're so fearless. I've seen

Krystal Fineman and her daughter working with their horses over at their indoor arena, and I swear, they don't do any better than you do, and they're using saddles and bridles."

Taylor perked up. "There's a riding arena near here?" she asked.

Axle grew animated. "Yes! The Fineman Wakes have a huge indoor riding arena, and Karla and her friend Mindy are always practicing. They have jumps, and they do dressage and pleasure riding, too. Sometimes Lucy Baxter from the Lazy B arranges to take her guests over to use the arena for riding lessons. Say, I've got an idea. This weekend is the first big outdoor picnic for the Lazy B guests. It's a huge fundraiser. I'm sure they'd love to have us come. After all, we'd be helping them raise money. What do you say?"

Taylor's heart pounded with excitement. An indoor riding arena with horses available for guests and girls who did dressage? She could hardly contain herself. "That's a wonderful idea. I'd love to meet other horse people in the area. Especially if this project is going to take us weeks instead of days." And she would have access to dozens of people who knew the Garrisons. She'd be sure to learn some juicy gossip there.

"Fantastic," said Axel. For the first time since they started working together, he seemed truly happy.

Taylor said, "I just have one question."

"Okay," said Axel. "What is it?"

"Do they have any alpacas?"

Axel burst out laughing. "No, they do not."

"Fantastic," said Taylor. "In that case, let's go buy me a printer so I can get more work done tonight, and we will have a beautiful day playing in the arena tomorrow."

"That sounds perfect. Thank you for wanting to go. I was really worried at first that you would hate the outdoor life from the way you were dressed and all. Plus, I thought you were a guy."

"I know," said Taylor. "You told me that when I arrived."

"But I don't care anymore. In fact, I couldn't be happier that my father sent a girl who's so cute and smart and actually enjoys my animals as much as I do."

Taylor was surprised. She turned and looked at him in time to see a hot blush creep up his cheekbones. Axel kept his eyes on the road for the rest of the drive into town. Taylor smiled to herself because she could tell that he hadn't meant to say any of those personal things to her. Maybe he was having trouble maintaining his hostility as well.

Chapter Fourteen

Sunday, April 10

STUCK IN THE WILDS OF COLORADO, Taylor did not expect the large-scale organization that greeted them as they drove towards the Victorian home of Krystal Fineman's family. Young people in bright orange vests directed the arriving vehicles toward a parking lot. Two large buses were already parked at the far end of the graveled area. The big white house was decorated with balloons and colorful swags of fabric. It reminded Taylor of a political campaign, but no candidate's name was in evidence. Somewhere behind the house, a live band was playing bluegrass. Once they got out of the SUV, it was easy to follow the line of arrivals and find the huge indoor arena. It stood like a horse lover's Coliseum, rising behind the older, smaller barn. The house itself was surrounded by lawn. The front garden was fenced, and everywhere you looked, there were signs that children lived and played here.

Taylor inhaled deeply of the fresh April morning. "This is my idea of heaven. You can smell the horses in the air."

Axel laughed softly. "Yes, I guess you could say that. Horses, and a few other things related to horses."

Taylor gave him a look.

Axel held up both hands. "I meant the alfalfa," he said defensively.

"You'd better mean alfalfa," she teased. "No man who shelters alpaca bile has a right to complain about manure."

Axel gave a short bark of a laugh. "Ha!" Then he sniffed the air again. "My favorite aroma is the hotdogs on the broiler and...." He paused to sniff again. "What is that enticing aroma? Something from my childhood."

It was Taylor's turn to laugh. "You have sophisticated tastes," she said sarcastically. "You're smelling cotton candy. They must have one of those machines. Oh, look over there." She pointed to an area west of the arena where several white tents had been set up to accommodate fundraising booths. One of them was indeed selling cotton candy, made on the spot. And for an extra nickel, the children were allowed to collect the delectable treat on their own paper cone.

Taylor's eyes shone with excitement. "This is terrific," she said. "This setup would make my mother jealous. What are they raising money for?"

Axel nodded toward a banner strung across the arena's front opening. "Zachary King's favorite charity," he said. The banner portrayed a cherubic face cheek to cheek with a horse's muzzle, along with the words, "Special Riders, Special Horses." Beneath that, in smaller print, was a statement that all the proceeds of the weekend's activities would go to support special needs children who came to the ranch to learn to ride. Axel added, "Zachary's the foreman here."

Taylor didn't want to admit it, but she was delighted by the arena, the horses, and the fundraising booths. The attendees were a mixed bag, from the looks of the vehicles in the parking lot,. A third appeared to be working ranch vehicles. Another third were high-end luxury rides, the kind she was used to seeing at her mother's fanciest affairs. And the rest were somewhere in between.

"Come on over here," said Axel. "Let's buy some tickets."

Behind a red-and-white checkered tablecloth sat two girls dressed in their finest riding apparel. Axel introduced them. "Hi, Karla. Hi, Mindy. This is my friend, Taylor. She came out from New York to help me write a biography about my father. Taylor, this is Karla Fineman Wake, the young equestrienne I was telling you about. And her friend Mindy. Gosh, you girls must be getting ready to graduate this year, right?"

His question elicited giggles from Mindy. Quiet Karla's darker hair, hazel eyes, and somber expression gave her more presence even though Mindy was taller by six inches.

"That's right," said Karla, her gaze flicking to Taylor and then back to Axel. "We'll be graduating in June. It's kind of sad, really. Mindy and I never wanted high school to end."

Taylor was puzzled. "Gee, most young people can't wait to go on to college. Surely you'll be doing that."

Karla nodded. "Yes, I guess you're right."

Mindy bounced up and down as she spoke. "OMG, it's so exciting! My parents finally agreed to let me go to the same school as Karla, and we'll be on the equestrian team, and we'll be competing at the national level! And we get to take our horses to campus, and—"

A tall, dark-haired man stepped up behind Mindy and laid a hand gently on her shoulder. "Easy, Mindy. No need to blindside our guests with your life story." He reached across the table and offered Axel his hand. "Good to see you, Axel. Great of you to come." He glanced around. "I don't see your cousins yet."

Axel shook hands. "I'm sure they'll show up, Kevin." Axel smiled. "They aren't totally despicable. And Zach's Special Horses charity is so important. Oh, forgive me. Let me introduce Taylor..." He hesitated.

Taylor supplied, "Hazen."

Axel continued. "She's helping me write a biography of my father."

When Kevin shifted his gaze to Taylor, she could feel the power of his personality behind it. "I'm Kevin Fineman Wake," he said. "You've already met my sister, Karla, and our friend, Mindy. You'll get to see them ride later."

Taylor shook his hand. "I'm looking forward to it. I'm having a huge case of arena envy."

"You ride?"

Mindy broke in, "Did you bring your horse?"

Kevin calmed her again. "Mindy, why don't you go help Megan with Kissie. Would you mind?"

"Not at all." Mindy seemed oblivious to Kevin's subtle manipulation. She wiggled her fingers at Taylor and Axel. "Can't wait to talk later." And she was off.

Karla continued selling tickets. A ten-year-old boy delivered a six-pack of Diet Coke to the table. As he trotted off, Karla muttered, "Thanks, Keegan."

Kevin motioned Axel and Taylor around behind the table, but it was clear to Taylor that he wanted to speak to Axel. She listened politely as the men began discussing local zoning matters and possible code violations pertaining to the Garrisons' building plans. After a few minutes, she lowered herself onto the chair vacated by Mindy and smiled politely at Karla, who pulled a can free from the six-pack and passed it to Taylor.

"Thanks. I'm so thirsty." She popped the top and took a sip. "Forgive me for asking, Karla, but have we met? You look so familiar."

Karla took a hundred-dollar bill from a middle-aged couple and handed them a pre-counted roll of green tickets. As they wandered away, she glanced sideways at Taylor and opened her own can of soda. "Depends," she said. "We may have met. Are you the same blue-haired Taylor Hazen who edged me out of first place in Hunter Jumper last August in Massachusetts?"

Taylor's jaw dropped, and her can of soda slipped through her fingers, bounced off her jeans, and fell to the ground.

Chapter Fifteen

AXEL FELT THE SODA SPLASH the calf of his jeans. A moment later, he was using a paper napkin to daub liquid off Taylor's anatomy.

"Are you planning to make a habit of this?" he asked softly. "Because maybe I should start packing a change of clothes when we go places."

Taylor laughed self-consciously, but Axel could hear the tension behind it.

Karla turned away to sell more tickets.

"What happened?" asked Kevin.

Taylor's discomfort rolled off her like heat from an oven.

Karla glanced up at her brother. "I startled her accidentally," she said. "It was my fault. Taylor, may I offer you a change of clothes?"

Taylor's chagrin evaporated. "Oh, that won't be necessary." Her gratitude was evident in her relieved expression. "So kind of you to offer. And hey, another great reason to drink Diet Coke, right? No sugary stickiness." She smiled up at Axel.

He knew something had just transpired, but he had no idea what it was. He'd ask her later.

Karla nodded in tacit agreement. "Offer stands if you need something later. Sorry I scared you."

Taylor patted Karla's shoulder. "Thanks." Then to Axel, "Gosh, let's go spend some of those tickets, shall we?"

Axel let Taylor lead the way, and soon they were ambling among the crowd, looking at brightly hued stuffed animals, giant striped suckers on sticks as thick as baseball bats, and dozens of other prizes that could be won with a lucky toss of a bean bag or by fooling someone at "Let Me Guess Your Weight." The booths were for charity, so once you bought your tickets, you were virtually guaranteed to win at least one prize. And of course, there was enough junk food to put a grown man in a coma.

Axel paused at one of the game booths. "Let's see how many bottles we can knock down." He passed a dozen tickets to the attendant, who handed him three baseballs in return.

"These things are rigged," said Taylor.

"Maybe at a carnival, but not here," said Axel. "This is a local fundraiser. No one wants to cheat you out of anything here. They've already got your money at the door." He was having fun, and he couldn't help it if it showed. But he could see that Taylor was still rattled. "So, what did Karla say to you back there?"

"Hmm? Er, nothing, not a thing. Really."

Axel took aim and let his first baseball fly. A tower of partially filled plastic bottles tumbled to the ground.

"I didn't see her make any sudden moves. What did she do, kick you under the table?" He let fly with the second ball, and another tower of bottles met their doom.

Taylor looked horrified. "She didn't kick me. She was very nice."

"She said she startled you." He threw the third baseball, and another six bottles fell to the ground.

The attendant looked sixteen, a skinny kid with a big voice. "We have a winner! Pick your prize!"

Axel waved an arm at the wall of prizes. "What would you like?"

Taylor looked flustered. "I don't care. Whatever you want."

Axel's forehead creased, but he let it go. "I picked this game because I had my eye on that magnificent pink and purple ostrich."

"There you go, sir. Congratulations!"

Axel took the puppet and struggled to manipulate the strings to make it walk. "That three-year-old over there makes it look so easy."

Taylor laughed, and Axel smiled. The tension was finally gone from her voice. "So, you think you can do better?" he asked.

Taylor slung her purse over one shoulder and took the puppet. "I daresay I can." She tilted the left wand, turning the ostrich's head to stare up at Axel with an accusing plastic eye the size of a billiard ball. The toy was so tall, she had to hold her arms out straight to use the controls. She moved her hands in a graceful pattern that soon had the ostrich striding through the crowd.

Axel said, "I'm impressed! You're really good at that."

Taylor gave him a teasing look. "I'll have you know I spent many wonderful hours at an arcade in my youth. Every chance I got, I would go pump quarters into machines or throw darts at strange boards, and I collected stuffed animals like they were stock options. I truly had a misspent youth. And then puberty hit and my parents insisted that I actually go to high school and college, and you know, all that stuff."

Axel laughed. "I cannot imagine my father ever letting me spend an hour or two at a games arcade pushing quarters into the machines. My dad thinks about money all the time. He's constantly worried about how I'm going to make my share. And I just want to write novels and take care of animals. Do you think that's wrong?"

Taylor's expression softened. "No. I think it's rather romantic actually. And if you can afford it, why not take the time to perfect your art? I have a brother studying painting in Paris right now."

Axel raised a brow. "Really? What does your father have to say about that?"

Taylor rolled her eyes at him. "You already know the answer to that. Our fathers seem to be a matched set."

Axel nodded but said nothing. That was exactly what he was worried about. His previous concerns returned full force. What if the toast Lester had made at the wedding in November had been another contest with Rudy? What were his father's motives? Why did he really send Taylor to help write his biography? Lost in thought, Axel realized suddenly that he couldn't see Taylor. There were so many people milling about the booths that he'd lost sight of her. "Taylor? Taylor, where did you go? Don't run away with my ostrich, girl."

From somewhere ahead of him he could hear the tinkle of a laugh, and it made him smile. There it was, the real little girl inside Taylor. Whatever else was going on with her taking a job that was far beneath her, whatever Karla had managed to say to throw her into a tizzy, all of that fell away when he heard her laugh. He would save the heavy questions for later. For now, it was enough that the sun was shining and he was spending a beautiful spring day with an equally beautiful young woman.

♡

Taylor congratulated herself on steering Axel clear of the Karla conversation. How could she have failed to remember the competitive young rider who nearly beat her at the Massachusetts horse show? And what a fool she'd been to think she could attend an event at a major horse facility like the Rocking Eagle and not run into at least one other national competitor? But Karla was so young.

That's why she hadn't recognized her. She'd assumed her competition at that event was her own age.

Now she wondered if Karla would say something to Axel about who she was. That was what had rattled her so badly. Her cover could have been blown in an instant. But lucky for her, Karla seemed more than decent about it. She even came up with an excuse for her. If it weren't for needing to spy on Axel, Taylor would drop the whole facade and give herself a chance to get to know the Fineman Wakes. They were obviously a family of substance. And the Fineman money was deeply rooted in Colorado. Of course! The hospital bore their name. She was certain now that everywhere she looked, she'd see the Fineman name. Her father had sent her out here to spy on a friend of the local jet set. What on Earth was he thinking? How could she keep her mission a secret in this environment?

She'd been looking forward to the opportunity to ride in the huge arena, but now she didn't dare. If she got on a horse that afternoon, Karla would certainly feel she had the right to chat with her about their competitions, and Axel would overhear and figure out that she wasn't some poor starving secretary looking for work after all.

Or did he already have it all figured out? He was sharp as a tack. And kind and generous. And gorgeous. Oh Lord, was he gorgeous! She would have to work extra hard this week. She needed dirt on Lester Garrison so she could pack up and go home to her own horse and put all of this behind her.

But why did that thought make her so sad?

Chapter Sixteen

AXEL WAS SURPRISED TO REALIZE how much fun he was having. Hadn't he just decided Friday night that he was going to razz Taylor and think up chores for her to do to keep her out of his hair? And here he was, following her around like a love-struck puppy, admiring her puppeteering skills. Darn his father, anyway. With every passing hour, Axel was more certain that Taylor was sent to seduce him into marriage, just to gratify his father's ego.

The problem was that Axel really liked her. A lot. He loved watching her move. He loved the sound of her laugh. And he loved the fact that she rode Thunder bareback and adored his reindeer herd.

He would obviously have to do some soul-searching. Meanwhile, maybe he could pursue his original plan of keeping her busy with make-work while he dove back into his novel. He smirked at the memory of the chapter he'd written the night before. He was taking all his frustrations about Taylor out on the written page, and his Great American Novel was beginning to sound like a romantic comedy. How could he resist? He had to put the mud fight and the alpaca spit into the book. And Taylor had already given him another attack of clumsiness to include when he got back to his computer.

Still, something about the exchange between her and Karla had upset her, and he couldn't help but wonder what it was.

Taylor tugged at his sleeve. "Hey, Earth to Axel."

"Hmm? What is it?"

"I said, I need to find a quiet spot to make a phone call. Any suggestions?"

"Oh, sure. Head around to the front of the house. There's a beautiful porch and swing there. It's probably quiet, since everyone is back here. Is everything okay?"

She gave him a casual shrug. "Everything's fine. I just need to check up on a…a friend. I won't be long."

Her last sentence made it clear he wasn't invited to eavesdrop on the conversation. But that was okay. He decided it was the perfect opportunity to touch base with Karla and find out what had happened at the ticket table.

He returned to the table, but instead of Karla, he found Kevin's wife Megan, counting money while young Keegan used a Labrador retriever's snout as a spool around which to roll tickets.

Megan was saying, "Not too tight, Keegan. Creamy needs to breathe." She looked up as Axel stopped in front of the table. "Out of tickets so soon?"

Axel smiled. "No, not yet. I expected to find Karla here."

"She's inside the arena, getting ready to ride. Anything I can help you with?"

Axel shook his head. "It's nothing serious. I just wanted to talk to her about a mutual friend. I'll be back when I need more tickets."

He headed inside, and sure enough, he spotted Karla right away. She struck a fine figure in her helmet, jacket, and boots. He waved at her. "Looking good, Karla."

"Thanks, Mr. Garrison."

"You know, with all the Garrisons in Eagle's Toe, you could call me Axel if you want."

Karla almost smiled. "If your cousins rub you too far the wrong way, you could change your name."

Axel gave her a teasing look. "That is very deep advice coming from someone so young."

Karla stroked her horse's nose. "What can I say? I guess I'm deep."

"Speaking of which," said Axel, "would you be betraying a secret if you told me what made Taylor spill her soda?"

Karla looked him up and down, and Axel had the definite feeling that she was examining him with some kind of x-ray vision. He'd heard stories about her troubled past, though seeing her decked out and ready for a ride made it hard to believe that she'd ever had a bad day in her life. But she was definitely taking stock of him before she answered.

At last, she said, "Seeing as how you think your eighty acres are better off in a natural state than covered with driveways and swimming pools, I guess it's okay to trust you. I kind of surprised Taylor because I remembered competing against her at a Massachusetts horse show last year. I don't know why she spilled her soda. I mean, she won the competition on that flashy warmblood of hers. Edged us out." She kissed her horse's nose. "So why all the drama? Excuse me, they're ready for me in the ring." She led her horse away.

Axel nodded. "Have fun." He stood for a few moments, watching Karla swing effortlessly up on the back of her horse. She looked like a million bucks astride her perfectly groomed mount. Or maybe a billion, considering how much family money was behind her.

So how could a hired secretary manage to afford a flashy horse and a life of competitive equestrian events? Axel felt a knot of suspicion balling in his gut. It was time to have a little chat with Taylor.

He strode like a man on a mission toward the front of the Victorian house. His mind raced through the possibilities. Had she duped his father? No, that didn't seem likely. If she was wealthy, she'd fit right in with his crowd. Why pretend to be otherwise? Then again, if Lester had sent her out here to seduce him into getting married, the whole secretary act could be for Axel's benefit. It was just a ruse to get her into his life and maybe into his bed, if that was indeed what his father was working on. Whatever was going on, he needed answers, and he needed them fast, because he was falling for Taylor in a big way.

He slowed as he reached the back gate of the little fence that surrounded the lawn. Kids and dogs required that he carefully latch the gate behind himself, and he did so. The grass muffled his steps as he moved along the side of the house toward the front porch. He could hear Taylor talking, and he slowed even further, hoping to get an idea of who she was talking to.

"Yes," she said. "And how was your day, Jackson? Did you have a good morning? You'd better not be flirting with all the girls, you stud. We've talked about that, remember? I have ways of stopping your flirtatious behavior. Yes, yes, I love you very much, you rascal."

Axel stopped cold. He felt like the ground had just dropped away beneath him. It didn't matter whether he was falling for Taylor or not,. She obviously had no interest in him. Her tone of voice made it clear that she was completely enamored of some guy named Jackson.

Chapter Seventeen

TAYLOR FINALLY HUNG UP AND decided it was time to get back to Axel. Now that she knew Jackson was okay, she could relax and enjoy the rest of their afternoon.

She spotted him at the cotton candy booth, stuffing a long pink strip of gooey sugar into his mouth. She sneaked up on him and announced, "Please tell me that's not your secret to staying in such great shape."

He glanced down at her and shrugged. "Sometimes you need comfort food."

Taylor's gaze shot left, then right. "Is something wrong?"

"Yes. They don't put nearly enough candy on these cones." His tone was distant, matter-of-fact.

Taylor was puzzled. "Okay, where's the guy I came with? You know, the one who was having a good time about ten minutes ago?"

Axel dumped the empty cone into a trash can and pulled a paper towel off a roll to wipe the sticky off his hands. "Nothing is getting written," he said. "We're wasting time, playing all morning, when we should be focused on getting this biography done."

Taylor couldn't figure him out. She'd been sure they were hitting it off. But now he was cold and distant and irritated. Well, if he had crazy mood swings, she was glad to find out now so she could stop thinking about how attractive he was all night.

Even so, it hurt her feelings that he had turned all business for some reason. "Well, maybe we should just leave and get back to work."

"Fine."

"Fine." She followed him back to his SUV. By the time they reached the highway, she decided it was for the best. After all, she wanted to get this done and go beat the crap out of her brother for accepting the vice presidency that was supposed to be hers.

Taylor had brought her laptop with her that morning because she couldn't stand the thought of leaving it in the hotel room. She took it into the cabin but left her purse in the car. No one was going to steal it out here. She set the computer up on the table in the cabin and busied herself with opening the biography file while Axel poured them each a cup of coffee. Part of her longed to be watching Karla ride at the fundraiser, but maybe she'd been having too much fun with Axel to dig up any dirt. She said, "Why don't we try something different?"

"Such as?"

She settled back in her chair. "I'll ask questions, and then I'll type your responses." She sipped her coffee.

Axel seemed impatient. "I'm a writer," he said. "If my fingers are on a keyboard, the words flow like crazy. But just sitting face to face with you? The words get all jumbled up. I can barely talk."

"Gee, thanks." Taylor preened, running her fingers through her blue hair as if it were as long as Rapunzel's.

Axel smiled begrudgingly. "You're welcome." Then he stood up. "Okay, let's give it a try. Ask away."

Taylor lifted her gaze to the ceiling. Even though he still seemed standoffish, at least he was willing to work. "Let me see." She typed her question as she asked it. "What is your fondest memory of your father?"

It wasn't a question that would elicit the dirt her own father wanted, but hey, she couldn't start out by asking where the family skeletons were buried.

Axel strolled to and fro, thumbs hooked on his jeans pockets. Taylor had to force herself to look at the computer. The sight of Axel in motion was captivating, and she still couldn't figure out why his attitude toward her had changed. She struggled to focus on the screen as Axel narrated.

"Easy one," he said. "When I was twelve, I went away to school. Pawling was only two hours away by train but at that age, it felt like I was a world away. It was my first year at prep school, or it was supposed to be. I was miserable and afraid to admit it. I was the oldest in my family, so there was no big brother ahead of me to pave the way or look out for me. I finally told my mother I wanted to come home. She said she had to discuss it with Dad, and I figured, that was the end of that.

No way would he understand. All he'd talked about the summer before was how great the place was and how it would get me into any college I wanted. Well, I was twelve. I wasn't thinking about college. That was way too far in the future.

"So I went back to my room and tried to hide from my roommate by burying my nose in a book. And at ten p.m. there was a huge ruckus in front of our residence hall. Horns blasting, headlights flashing on and off. That was supposed to be lights-out time. So of course we were all awake. We opened the dorm window to see what was going on, and there was Dad, looking for me. When he spotted me, he said, 'Pack your bag. We're leaving.'

"We drove back home that very night. He ranted about the school all the way. He was furious with them but not mad at me. He went on and on about how they'd assured him I would have a positive experience. Make new friends, with a comforting adult presence, no *Lord of the Flies* nonsense. The next day, he was on the phone for hours, reading them the riot act. It was the first time in my life I'd ever seen him go to bat for me." He stopped and stared down at the floor.

Taylor was typing as fast as she could. "That's a great story. See? This method could work. What happened after that? Did you have to go back to prep school?"

"Not that year. My folks hired a couple of private tutors so I'd be prepared to go back a year later. By the time I was thirteen, I was ready. But I was a legend when I went back. All the boys who'd ignored me the year before thought my father was the greatest, and they all wanted to be my friend. Amazing."

Taylor nodded. "So he saved you twice in one night."

Axel pointed a finger at her. "That's it exactly! And his complaints to the school administration had brought about some changes on campus, too. The other boys all felt they'd benefitted from him pulling me out."

Taylor stopped typing long enough take another sip of coffee. "That was good. Okay, let's try another question." She hesitated, wondering if it was too soon. But she needed negative stuff. She forged ahead, because she was missing Jackson like crazy and no herd of reindeer could fill that void. She cleared her throat. "All right. Let's go to the other end of the spectrum." She started typing and talking at the same time, mostly to avoid looking at Axel. "What was the worst moment you ever had with your father?"

Axel pulled a chair around so he could straddle it and rested his arms on the back. "That's not as easy to talk about."

Silence.

Taylor was worried that he would clam up. She waited, afraid to push too hard. She was just about to think of a new question when Axel spoke.

"The day he married Bambi."

"His new wife?"

"Yes. We all felt it was too soon and too stupid. She's obviously a gold digger. She's my age, for God's sake. I just don't get it." More silence.

Taylor's fingers hovered over the keys, waiting. At last, she nudged. "Did you and your father argue about it?"

"Oh, many times. The last time was the worst. He told me I was wasting my life trying to be a writer. He said I should do something that would make money. So I decided it was time to come out west for a while. Get reacquainted with my cousins." He snorted but did not elaborate.

"Well, this is a great start," said Taylor. "Let's see if I can come up with another productive question."

Axel rested his chin on his arms. "I think it's my turn," he said.

Taylor pulled her hands back from the laptop. "Your turn?"

"To ask a question."

She shrugged. "Oh. Okay." What harm could it do? As long as he kept talking and she was getting closer to her goal, fine, let him ask a question.

Axel's eyes seemed to bore right through her. "I need to know the answer to this question if we're going to continue working together."

"Fine," said Taylor, wondering what sort of question could make or break their arrangement. Did he suspect her true motives? Had he heard something from his siblings in New York? But what would they know? How could any of them know about her deal with her father? She braced herself for the worst. "Ask away."

Axel narrowed his eyes and peered at her. "Who is Jackson?"

Chapter Eighteen

TAYLOR BLINKED AT HIM, wondering if she'd heard correctly. "Jackson?"

"Don't pretend you don't know what I'm talking about. Every day when I drop you off at the Cattleman's, I can see you in my rearview mirror, phone in hand. You're making a call before you even get inside. I didn't think much of it. But today, I...accidentally...overheard you saying his name on the phone. So, who is Jackson?"

Taylor wasn't sure what to say. Her mind raced, trying to determine why he felt it necessary to know about Jackson. "Is it important?"

Axel gazed out the window, then rubbed his forehead with one hand. "I'm starting to like having you around," he blurted. "But if there's another guy waiting for you in New York, then I should rein things in a bit. You know. Before I get too attached." He avoided her eyes but looked sideways at her, from toes to shoulders.

Taylor's head was spinning. She was pleased that Axel liked her, and then she was surprised that she was pleased. This hadn't been part of the original plan. The biggest surprise of all was the realization that she liked him, too. A lot. And every day that they spent together, sharing their feelings and their personal history, made her like him more and more. They had so much more in common than he realized. For a few moments, she scrambled mentally for the wisest answer. In the end, given Axel's love of animals, she decided the truth might actually fly.

"Jackson is my horse. A warmblood gelding and the love of my life. He lives in a stable in Central Park, and I call every day to check on his feed and his exercise. There you go. My secret's out. I'm a closet equestrienne."

Axel laughed with relief. "A horse? That's awesome."

"You think so?"

"Definitely. I thought you had a boyfriend checking up on you every day. You called him a stud."

Taylor made a face. "He still thinks he's a stallion. I don't want to destroy his illusions."

Axel's good mood had returned in spades. "I love that you have a horse. See? I knew you were an animal person. The way you took to the reindeer, and the way you rode Thunder, and the way you beat out Karla—" He bit off the rest of the sentence, but it was too late.

"You talked to Karla about me?"

Axel made an "eek" face. "Only because you were so rattled by something she said and I didn't want anything to ruin your day." He dropped his gaze to the floor. "Then I went ahead and took care of that part myself. I was sort of aggravated when I thought you were talking to another man. I'm really sorry. But I'm thrilled that you have a horse."

"Could you tell my father that? I mean, how it's awesome to have a horse?"

Axel spread his hands. "Any time. What's his number?"

Taylor felt a flutter of panic. She couldn't let him talk to her father. That would not be good. Either Pembroke would get impatient and ask for information about Lester from the source or Axel would find out she was supposed to be spying on him and his family. She needn't have worried, though. Axel had glossed over his request for contact information and rushed on with his own thoughts.

"You came out here to work with me on my father's biography, knowing it would take months and you had to leave your horse behind? That is terrible. I can't let you do that."

Taylor objected. "But I really need to do this. I'm trying to insure Jackson's future." *And get that corner office and a big, fat salary, even if I have to drag it out of my brother's clutches,* she added to herself.

Axel eyed her curiously. "I have one more question."

Taylor gulped. "Okay," she said warily.

"My father hired you to come out here and help me write this book. But how can you afford to keep a horse in New York City and wear Armani on a secretary's salary?"

"I'm not a secretary in real life," said Taylor. She was so relieved that his question was that easy to answer that her tongue took over and rushed on with, "Besides your father didn't hire me. Mine did." Then she gasped and covered her mouth with one hand when she realized what she'd just said.

Axel's jaw dropped.

Taylor pressed her lips into a thin line, hoping she wouldn't make another stupid mistake. But the cat was out of the bag.

Axel stood up and began to pace. "Let me get this straight. Your father sent you out here…but my father told me he was sending you…so your father and mine must be in cahoots on this deal."

Taylor winced. "Sort of. I guess. All I know is that my dad suggested me to your father when Lester wanted to send someone out here to help you write this biography."

"Why?"

Taylor slumped in her chair. She didn't want to tell Axel she was supposed to spy on him, but on the other hand, she didn't want to jeopardize the bond that was growing between them. Finally, she gave up. "Oh rats. All right. I'll tell you." She took a deep breath and began. "My dad, Pembroke Hazen, is trying to work a merger with one of your dad's companies, but lately, your dad has been dragging his feet. So my dad decided he should send me out here to get some dirt on your dad so he'll have leverage to use against Lester when they meet next Friday to finalize their deal."

Axel stared at her in disbelief. "He sent you out here to spy on me?"

Taylor made a puppy dog face. "I'm really sorry. That's how it started out. But I don't care about that anymore. Besides, Daddy betrayed me. He told me he'd give me the vacant vice presidency if I did this for him, and all the time, he was just trying to get me out of the way so he could give the job to my brother Don while I was gone."

Axel went to the cupboard and took down one of the several bags of cookies that now crammed his shelves. With his other hand, he reached into the small cupboard above the refrigerator and pulled down a pint of vodka. He set them both on the table. "I think we need fortification," he said. "Do you drink?"

Taylor's eyes widened. "Not really."

"That's okay. Cookies have the same effect, if you eat enough of them. But just in case…" He poured a dollop of vodka in her coffee, then a double dollop into his own. "Try it. You'd be surprised how good those cookies are with vodka. Besides, I need to tell you what I think is going on. Because frankly, I think our fathers have teamed up to pull a dirty trick on both of us."

Chapter Nineteen

AXEL BEGAN BY TELLING TAYLOR the story of the November wedding and his father's quasi-intoxicated toast.

Taylor munched a frosted animal cookie and washed it down with vodka-laced coffee. By the time Axel got to the part about the big fight on the ride home and his decision to take off for Colorado, Taylor was on her third cookie and had emptied her coffee mug.

"So you see," said Axel, adding a dollop of vodka to her mug with one hand and filling it with lukewarm coffee with the other, "I think we are both being manipulated by two masters of the art form."

Taylor chewed fast and swallowed more coffee so she could speak. "You mean, they wanted to throw us together on a long-term project so we would fall for each other and get married?"

"I don't have any proof, but I wouldn't put it past my father to do something like that. It has Garrison written all over it."

Taylor was beginning to feel a buzz from the vodka. She took another swallow, smacked her lips, then banged her mug on the table. "We can't let them win," she said.

"I agree." Axel took three cookies, two white-frosted elephants and a pink-frosted giraffe, and made a sandwich out of them. He crunched and munched and washed it all down with the last of his own coffee. He poured more vodka into his mug, then said, "I'm out of coffee."

Taylor shoved her mug toward him, sloshing some of its contents on the table. "Have some of mine."

He did so.

"We need a plan," said Taylor, enunciating her words carefully.

Axel nodded and chewed and swallowed and kept nodding until he could speak again. "I've got one. And I think it will serve them right."

Taylor blinked up at him. "Do tell."

"We're going to let them think their plan is working."

"It is working," said Taylor. "We really like each other." She belched. "A lot."

Axel belched louder, unable to resist the challenge. "I know. It's incredibly inconvenient, too, because I have a book to write."

"And I thought I was going to get a nice big fat salary and an office and a staff and buy a big farm upstate for Jackson."

Axel waved a hand. "I have eighty acres, and this is horse country. You've seen the barn. There's plenty of room. We'll bring Jackson out here so you can see him every day."

Taylor's eyes bulged. "Do you mean it?" Then her face fell. "I can't quite afford it, I'm afraid. Flying stables are expensive, and Daddy insists I work for mailroom wages."

Axel wagged a finger. "Don't worry about that. I'll pay for it."

"But, but, but I thought writers don't make any money."

"Remember my mother? Before she died, she made provisions for me and my siblings in her will. She brought her own money into the marriage. How do you think I was able to come out here and buy acreage and rescue livestock? I'd be happy to bring Jackson out for you."

Taylor bounced with excitement. "That would be wonderful! Oh, thank you so much." She sprang out of her chair and wrapped her arms around Axel.

He returned her embrace, and they stood there for several seconds, hugging and rocking back and forth. Taylor looked up at him and Axel looked down at her, and a second later, he leaned over and planted a soft kiss on her sweet lips. He wondered if she always tasted that good, or was it the vodka-and-cookie combination? It didn't matter. When she pulled his head even closer, inviting a deeper kiss, he suddenly realized that the biggest problem he was going to have would be refusing to get married within his father's time frame.

Then Taylor froze. "Wait. If I'm only going to be here another week, it's too much to bring Jackson out."

Axel rubbed her arms. "Now that I know he's a horse, I frankly want to have my competition where I can keep an eye on him. What's the stable's number?"

"My phone is in my purse. I left it in the car. I'll go get it."

77

On her way, she questioned the wisdom of bringing her horse to Colorado. She'd been so anxious to get back to New York. But that was because she missed Jackson. And now that her father had given her vice presidency to Don, what was the hurry? She would stay in Colorado a while longer than planned. Maybe a lot longer. And if her father didn't like it, too bad. Maybe it was time for her to start making her own decisions.

They spent the rest of the afternoon on the phone, making arrangements to transport Jackson to Eagle's Toe. Before Axel drove her back to town, they assessed the barn, deciding what Taylor might want to pick up at the Feed and Grain the next morning.

"I'll call the owner," said Axel. "He'll open up early for a big order." He scuffed his feet against the barn floor. "I guess I have to drive you back to town now."

Taylor was as reluctant as he sounded about leaving. "We did say we can't let them win. I guess we'll just have to be strong."

Axel cupped her cheek in one hand. "At least until we come up with a different plan of action." He marveled at how quickly this adorable thorn in his side had managed to work her way into his heart.

Taylor giggled.

A moment later, they were kissing again. When they came up for air, Taylor asked, "Are you sure you're okay to drive?"

"Our vodka was hours ago. I'm fine. The only buzz I've got is coming from you."

Taylor stamped her foot and pretended to whine. "This isn't what I'd planned at all. I was supposed to dig up some really good dirt on your father and go home to a big salary in the City and be a pampered equestrian princess."

Axel rubbed his nose against hers. "Don't worry. You can be a pampered equestrian princess in Colorado. And as for dirt on my father? Let me give that some thought." He felt a flicker of an idea forming in the back of his mind, but with Taylor within kissing distance, he couldn't think straight. "I've got to get you back to the hotel before we do something that would make our fathers very happy."

Taylor laughed out loud. "That sounded so totally twisted, I can't even argue with you."

Axel was beaming when he pulled under the Cattleman's portico. "We can get Jackson's stall ready tomorrow. The Feed and Grain is across the street. When I pick you up in the morning, we can collect whatever you need and take it with us. How's that sound?"

Taylor looked thrilled. "How can I ever thank you?" She leaned across the seat and planted a warm goodbye kiss on his lips. "See you tomorrow." She hefted her purse and computer bag and got out of the SUV.

When she turned at the entrance to wave goodbye, Axel was still staring after her, one hand pressed against his mouth. He was stunned by the fire that Taylor's kisses had lit inside him. He hadn't felt this way about a woman since…well, he couldn't remember anything similar to this, not since high school and those first mad crushes on the cheerleading squad.

He drove away from the Cattleman's and headed for The Nest, the little burger joint west of town. The cookies he'd consumed gurgled ominously inside. He needed real food. And he wanted to make a phone call. He needed information, the kind he could only get from his family.

He and his siblings had expended a great deal of energy telling their father how unwise he had been to marry Bambi. But none of them had ever seriously inquired about why he'd done it. If Lester had shared his reason with any of them, they hadn't listened. But Axel was pretty certain their father had clammed up when his children rebelled at his choice of a wife. Regardless of how he felt about his father's second marriage, it was time to call him and ask what the heck was going on where Taylor was concerned.

He wasn't prepared to have Bambi answer the phone.

"Hello? Garrison residence."

Axel sat for a moment, mouth open, trying to decide what to say.

"Axel? Is that you? Or did someone steal your cell phone?"

"Oh, uh, sorry, Bambi. I thought my father would answer. It must be eight o'clock there."

"He's not home yet. He has some big business meeting. Again." She sounded less than pleased. "Has he always been this obsessed with work?"

Axel grunted an affirmative. "Short answer? Yes. Didn't he warn you about that before you married him?" He fought to keep the sarcasm out of his voice, but didn't entirely succeed.

Bambi sighed heavily. Axel could visualize her on the other end of the line—tall, model thin, dark wavy hair probably drawn back in a low ponytail, hiding her beauty under sweatpants and a tee shirt. When she went out with Lester, she always dressed to the nines, but Axel had been surprised to discover that at home, she pulled on the fastest, easiest, and most comfortable apparel. He waited for her to berate him for his sarcasm.

She surprised him. "Look, Axel, I don't want us to be enemies. Remember, your father came after me. I didn't have any plans to marry anybody when I met him. Let's not hate each other, okay? I can't help it if he charmed my socks off."

Axel frowned at his phone. Was she holding out an olive branch? Maybe discovering that Lester was still committed one hundred and ten percent to his business interests had jolted her. Maybe she'd thought he would love her more than he loved his money. And maybe Axel's reindeer would fly next Christmas Eve.

"Sorry, Bambi. I don't want to be enemies either. It's just a shock to have your father marry a woman young enough to be his daughter."

"I can understand that," said Bambi. "And I admit, I thought we'd be spending more time together. Sometimes I feel like the fun part for him was the chase. Once we were married, he dove right back into his business. I was hoping we'd get to travel a bit, you know, maybe go somewhere interesting a few times a year? But after our honeymoon, that was it. He was all work and no travel." She paused, as if realizing her words might get back to Lester. "Don't get me wrong, I'm still very happy being Mrs. Lester Garrison. But like you said, there's a big difference in our ages. I guess I didn't think that part all the way through." She laughed softly. "But hey, you called for a reason. What can I do for you?"

Axel thought about hanging up and dialing his father's office, but he didn't want to ruin this chance to actually learn a few things from Bambi. "Did he tell you I'm writing his biography?"

"Oh yes, he mentioned something about that."

"Well, he sent me an editorial assistant who keeps asking questions I don't have answers to. Maybe you could help me with that."

"I'll help if I can."

Axel began to think he'd misjudged Bambi. Maybe she wasn't the evil gold digger they all thought she was. "Great. The question is…I hope you're not offended by this…why did Lester marry you? Sorry, I know that sounds terrible. But—"

"No problem." Bambi cut him off. "I know exactly why he married me. He fell in love with me the first time he saw me."

That hurt. Axel supposed his father still had enough life in him to love again after losing their mother, but he'd barely waited a year before he marched down the aisle with Bambi.

"Axel? Are you still there?"

"Yeah. My thoughts ran straight to my mother. It all just seemed to happen so fast."

"I can't argue with that," said Bambi. "Like I said, he swept me off my feet. But I know why. I figured it out the first time I saw your parents' wedding photo."

Axel tried to pull the image out of long-term memory, but all he could see was his mother that last week in the hospital, her head swathed in bandages, her face swollen and bruised from the plane crash. "I'm not sure what you mean."

Bambi's voice softened. "When your mother was my age, she looked exactly like me. Your father didn't stand a chance. When he met me, he fell in love with your mother all over again."

Axel was stunned. "I wasn't expecting that answer. My memories of my mother…. I can't get those last few weeks out of my mind. She was so badly injured."

"I understand. At first, it freaked me out. But Lester assured me that he loved me for more than my looks. I just hope that was true. He's been so distant lately. So wrapped up in his latest deal. He's constantly in meetings, and when he's home, he keeps getting business-related phone calls, some from a guy named Mulligan, some from his brother, and some from a guy with a weird name, like 'peanut' or 'hazelnut.' No. Hazen. That's who he's dealing with. Some billionaire named Hazen."

Axel nodded. "Yes, I know. I'm sort of acquainted with his daughter." He'd been right all along. His father was trying to get him hitched, and Axel had no doubt what the supposed merger was all about.

"Do you want me to have him call you when he gets home?"

"No, that's okay. You've answered all my questions."

"He could call tomorrow. I know he wants to make up after that big fight you two had."

"I'm expecting a horse tomorrow night." He recalled Karla's description. "A flashy warmblood named Jackson. So I'll be busy in the barn all day." The old man was planning a merger with Hazen, eh? Well, Axel would have a few things to say about that. "Don't worry. I plan to call Dad on Monday. I have a surprise for him."

Yes, indeed. Lester was in for a big surprise.

Chapter Twenty

AFTER AXEL DROPPED HER OFF, Taylor floated across the lobby. She couldn't decide what she was happier about, knowing that Axel returned her feelings or that Jackson would soon be with her in Colorado. Once she reached her suite, she ordered filet mignon and chocolate mousse from room service, then poured herself a tall tonic water on ice before settling in her favorite spot to watch the sunset. She was in a celebratory mood. The only thing better would be having Axel there to celebrate with her, but they'd agreed that they needed to be very careful about their time together. Taylor had never felt about a man the way she was yearning for Axel. Things could get very heated very fast, if they weren't careful.

Darn his father and that stupid wedding toast! If not for that, they could give in to their feelings whenever they wished. But maybe it was a good idea to wait a bit. She barely knew Axel, and yet she felt like they'd known each other all their lives. She just wanted to be wrapped in his arms all day. And all night. She found herself humming that old song, "I Only Want to Be With You."

As the sun painted the clouds orange over the western mountains, she pondered Axel's words in the barn. He'd been on the brink of a brilliant idea, she was sure. And she'd loved it when he said she could be a pampered equestrian princess in Colorado. She sighed and marveled at how much more beautiful the mountains looked this evening.

She heard a knock at the door. Her dinner had arrived. It was Cody again. He clearly wanted to be sure to bring her dinner every time since she'd given him that big tip the other night. After he left, grinning like he'd won the lottery, she settled on her sofa. She wasn't really hungry. She was still full of those afternoon cookies, but filet mignon seemed the thing to order when one was celebrating.

She was just about to cut into the steak when her phone rang. She glanced at it. "Daddy." She shook her head. She wasn't in the mood, not after he'd given her prize away to her brother. But she knew she couldn't enjoy her dinner if she had to call him later, so she picked up.

"Hello, Daddy." She wasn't at all prepared for Pembroke's opening salvo.

"Taylor! Why on Earth are you shipping your horse to Colorado?"

Taylor's mouth opened, but nothing came out as a thousand questions raced for the gate and none found traction. At last, she sputtered, "How in the world could you possibly know about me bringing Jackson out here, when the decision was only made five hours ago?"

Then she had a terrible thought. "Did you have cameras planted in Axel's cabin?"

Pembroke walked back his tirade. "No, of course not. So you're on a first name basis at last, eh? He must be talking to you finally instead of giving zoo tours."

"Rescued alpacas and a herd of reindeer do not constitute a zoo. He's an animal lover, and frankly, I admire him for that, even if he is the son of your business adversary." She wondered what else she should say. She wasn't about to tell her father about her growing affection for Axel. And she certainly wasn't going to tell him about their shared kisses or her very hot dreams about him. She traced a finger along the arm of the sofa. "Of course he's talking to me. But I've had to work hard to gain his trust. A person doesn't bare his soul to a stranger. I finally came up with a method to get information about his father. Now tell me how you know about my plans for Jackson?"

Pembroke slipped into his "Daddy-loves-you" voice. "Oh, sweetheart, I'm your father. I know a lot of things about you almost before they happen. Parental instincts."

Taylor took a sip of tonic water. The bubbles tickled her nose. "Why don't I believe you?"

His voice turned gruff. "Just because I think you should spend more time on learning the family business than on playing with horses doesn't mean I don't want you to be happy. And Jackson makes you happy. So I've been keeping tabs on him for you."

Taylor made a face at the phone. "You mean you bribed one of the stable hands to keep you informed of any new developments."

Pembroke chuckled. "My little girl is a chip off the old block. Suspicious and cynical. I'm so proud."

"Oh, yes, I'm sure you are. If you're so proud of me, why did you want to get rid of me? Oh wait, that's right. You wanted me out of the way so you could give Donald my vice presidency."

"Good heavens, Taylor. What's got into you? I told you I'd find one for you, too. Just because I had already planned to bring Don back from San Francisco doesn't mean you won't be rewarded for doing my dirty work. Keep your eyes on the prize, sweetheart. Use your feminine wiles on him. Flirt if you have to."

Taylor nearly choked on her tonic water. She couldn't believe her father had just said that! It totally backed up Axel's theory about why she'd been sent to Eagle's Toe. She swished her glass and the ice cubes tinkled. "If that's your plan, Dad, you may be out of luck. I think he's immune to that kind of thing. All he thinks about is rescuing more animals." She covered her mouth to muffle her giggle.

"I thought he wanted to be a writer."

"He does. He is. I've seen the novel he's working on," she fibbed. Well, she'd seen the stack of manuscript pages on the kitchen counter. "It's really good. But unlike some men I know," she said pointedly, "he has more than one interest in life."

"So he loves animals. That should give you two a lot in common. Keep at it, Taylor. I need that info by Friday. Did you learn anything today?"

"Nothing that would help your cause. So far, he just says nice things about his dad. But I think he's warming up to me." She fought to keep the smile out of her voice. "Bringing Jackson to Colorado was his idea."

"You don't say. Well, don't get so wrapped up in your horse that you forget I need the goods on Lester by Friday. I have to go now. I have some associates coming for drinks at nine-thirty. Bye-bye."

Taylor hung up, then dialed another number immediately. She wanted to know who at the stable was reporting to her father. The filet mignon looked divine, but first things first. She needed to talk to the stable manager. He lived on-site, in an apartment adjacent to the facility.

"Hello, Roger? It's Taylor Hazen."

"Checking on your boy, eh? Nothing to worry about, Miss Hazen. Jackson is sleek and sassy, and we're getting everything ready for his flight to Colorado tomorrow."

"Great. I'm so glad. I know you take great care of him."

"That's a relief. When you decided to fly him to Colorado, I was afraid someone here had displeased you."

"Not at all. Don't worry, Roger. When I come home, Jackson will come with me. But I do have a question."

"Fire away."

"Did you get a call from my father today asking about Jackson?"

"No, not me. No message, either. And I'd remember because he has never called me before, not ever."

"Is it possible that one of the grooms might have talked to him about Jackson coming to Colorado?"

"No way. No one could have told him anything because I'm the only one who knows about it. I've been handling all the trip details myself."

"Thank you, Roger. You know how much I appreciate your hard work." Taylor hung up. More and more curious. How had her father found out? And why had he lied to her?

Chapter Twenty-One

TAYLOR TRIED CALLING AXEL to fill him in on her conversation with her father, but the call wouldn't go through. And when she texted him, she got a message that the text failed. He must have turned off his phone. He'd said something about shutting out the world when he was writing. Frustrated, she sent him an email, but she didn't know if or when he would see it.

Her frustration was mounting, in more ways than one. The more she thought about him, the more she wished she could get another rental car and just drive up to the darn cabin. But the road was still a mess. His SUV had a six-inch layer of mud spatter all over the bottom half and partway up the hood. Besides, the only place to rent a car in town was at Brady's garage, and he'd been the one who hauled her mud-slogged car down off the mountain. No way he'd trust her with one of his cars after that.

She would have to wait until morning.

She cast a baleful eye at her little filet mignon. It was cold. She investigated behind the bar. Yes, there was a microwave. Although she cringed at the thought of microwaving such a fine cut of meat, she decided it would be okay to warm it up a tad. Thirty seconds later, she was finally able to curl up on her sofa with her dinner. The sun was lowering itself slowly behind the mountain, like a person sinking with relief into a tub of hot water. Or maybe cold water, since the mountains were still covered with snow.

Halfway through her chocolate mousse she opened her laptop and stared at the screen. She no longer wanted to find any real dirt on Lester.

How could she, when all she wanted was to snuggle in the arms of his son? Then she had a flash of inspiration. She would make stuff up! She spooned mousse into her mouth and held the spoon there with her tongue as her fingers flew across the keys. Since these notes would go to her father in the form of an email, she didn't have to make it sound like a biography. That was Axel's department.

"Lester once had a controlling interest in a casino in Atlantic City, so it looks like he had business associates in the Mafia. Not sure that's what they still call themselves, but a couple of them had criminal records. Axel says not to worry about that, but he won't put their real names in the biography, because there were rumors that Lester's business partner died under suspicious circumstances."

She laughed out loud. This was fun. After all, Daddy wanted dirt on Lester, and there wasn't any, but what Daddy wants, Daddy gets. And that paragraph alone should give her father pause. So she kept going. What else would really put her father off?

"It seems that Lester's finances may be shaky. He's being audited and Axel thinks it's worse than Lester makes it sound because Lester won't share any details. Axel has his own money. His mother left it to him. He plans to spend every penny on his eighty-acre animal rescue farm."

Oh, she hadn't said anything about Lester's wife yet. She stared at the ceiling for a while, then began typing again.

"Lester's wife, Bambi, likes expensive cars and designer clothes. She has half a million dollars in handbags so far. And she likes to send her favorite politicians on junkets to Europe." She paused. That sounded pretty over the top. She added, "Of course, they have to be careful, so they award the trips to the politicians' kids as educational scholarships." There. That sounded like something a crafty person would think of.

She almost hit send, but decided she'd better run the email past Axel first. What if she'd accidentally stumbled on a real family secret? She didn't want to do that. She turned off her laptop and moved into the bedroom. She'd find a nice, romantic movie on TV and spend the rest of the night thinking about Axel. Maybe she'd make a list of questions for him. Question number one: How long before that new house is built? Number two: Where do you want to go on our honeymoon?

Then she had a fit of giggles. She snuggled up around a large pillow, wondering how she'd ever thought Axel was a country bumpkin.

Chapter Twenty-Two

Monday, April 11

THE NEXT MORNING, TAYLOR COULD hardly wait for Axel to pick her up. She climbed into the SUV and opened her laptop.

"I almost sent this disinformation to my father before showing it to you," she said. "But then I wondered if any of it was true. I mean, we want to mess with them, but I didn't want to get your father in any real trouble." Or get herself in any real trouble with Axel.

He skimmed through the email, chuckling here and there. At the end, he said, "Take out the part about Bambi. I had a real interesting phone call with her yesterday. I don't want to say anything negative about her."

Taylor deleted the paragraph about Bambi. "Shall I hit send?"

"Definitely," said Axel. "That will give them something to talk about besides us."

"By the way, when I called my dad to check in last night, he already knew we were flying Jackson to Colorado! My stable manager swears there's not a leak at his end."

"The leak might have been Bambi. I told her I was expecting a horse this afternoon. She probably called my father and filled him in."

Taylor shook her head in disgust. "And he probably called *my* father and told him."

"We could be totally off base," said Axel thoughtfully, "but I don't think we are. Bambi said the CEO Dad was spending all his time with is named Hazen."

"Aha! We've caught them in the act!"

"Yes. Now if only we knew what the act was all about."

"Are you getting cold feet? I thought you said you were sure you're father was trying to set us up."

"Yes, and I'm still sure that's a part of it. But why would *your* father jump in with both feet? I mean, I'm a great catch and all, but I'm no Warren Buffet."

Taylor gave him a sarcastic look. "You're thinking this is about you and your father. What if it's all on my side? I told you he lied to me about the job he was going to give me. My father thinks that because I'm a girl, I don't have a head for business. He's done this to me before. He sends me away when he wants to give one of my brothers a big gift or a huge career boost. I complain, and he pats me on the head and sends me to equestrian camp. Of course, then he turns around and blames me for my own lack of business progress by telling me I spend too much time with my horse." She made a disgusted noise.

"Speaking of horses," said Axel, pointing through the windshield, "Mr. Parker just arrived to open the Feed and Grain for us. Hey, where's your purse?"

"Rats! I left it in my room."

"Don't worry. I'll put everything on my credit card, and you can pay me back later." He started the SUV and pulled up in front of the Feed and Grain across the street.

Parker greeted her with his hand extended. "Nice to meet you, young lady." Taylor figured he must be seventy at least, and he had that wrinkled, tan look sported by men who'd spent half their lives outdoors. Maybe more than half, if they were sleeping rough. But he also had an air of quality about him. "I don't open early for just anybody," he said. "But for the man who saved Lucy Baxter's Lazy B? I'm all over that. Come on in."

Taylor walked in the door and took a deep breath. The smell of leather tack and horse treats and fly traps made her giddy. She'd always loved buying tack, and since she wasn't sure how much of Jackson's would come with him, she let herself splurge.

Axel browsed as she shopped, a bemused look on his face.

"Don't you have any English saddles?" Taylor asked Mr. Parker.

Axel looked up from a display of local newspapers with livestock ads in them. He pulled two out of the box and said, "I think they're sending his saddle with him. That's what the guy on the phone said."

"If my stable manager gets it all together," said Taylor, slightly annoyed that Axel would derail her spending spree with logic.

But Axel just grinned at her. "If you want to buy a new saddle, why not look at the lightweight western saddles? Then you'll have one as a souvenir from Colorado."

Taylor clapped her hands together. "Great idea! And certainly a celebratory saddle pad is in order."

"Most definitely. You'll need one to go with the new saddle."

Now she could tell he was just helping her spend money, and she was loving it.

When they collected everything she couldn't live without, Axel pulled out his credit card at the counter.

"I'll pay you back as soon as I get some cash," said Taylor.

"That sounds fair. In fact, if it makes you feel better, I'll let you pay for his hay as well."

Taylor laughed, her eyes sparkling. "Definitely. Thank you so much."

Mr. Parker asked, "Is that road of yours passable? I can have hay delivered tomorrow."

Axel grinned and nodded. "It's firming up pretty good. Delivery would be nice. I'll start loading these things in the Expedition."

"You need a bale in the back for tonight?"

Taylor popped up, "Yes, please."

Once the SUV was loaded, Axel reminded Taylor that it would be cooler at the cabin. He stopped at the Cattleman's so she could retrieve her purse and a jacket as well. She set her purse on the back seat and tossed her jacket over it.

When they got to the cabin, they took their time preparing Jackson's stall. Every hour, Taylor's phone would ping with a text from the flight attendants, updating her on their progress and Jackson's well-being. By noon, everything was ready.

"I guess we'd better work on the biography," said Axel.

"Do you think it's a real project?" asked Taylor. "Or just a means to an end? Getting us together?"

Axel pulled straw out of her hair. "That's a good question," he said huskily. "Maybe we should put our heads together and see if we can figure this out." He leaned in for a kiss.

Taylor enjoyed the feel of his lips against hers until her body tried to convince her that the hay scattered on the floor was a fine substitute for a mattress. Then she pushed him gently away.

She panted, "I thought the whole point was to make sure your father can't make good on his toast."

Axel groaned. "I almost forgot." He cleared his throat. "I'm going out to check on the reindeer. I need a break."

"Don't forget to give them treats for me, too. I'm going inside. It's clouding over, and without the sun, it's chilly out here."

Axel eyed her with mock shrewdness. "I see that my reindeer have worked their charms on you."

Taylor made a face. "Just because I'm thinking they'll make great company for Jackson...."

Axel chuckled. "I won't be long. I need some fresh air to clear my head."

"I'll make us some tea." She stopped at the SUV to retrieve her computer and her purse. Once inside, she set the computer bag on the table and her purse on the floor. The cabin was warm, so she slipped her jacket off and draped it over her purse. Then she pulled two mugs off the kitchen shelf and set the kettle on the stove.

As she waited for the kettle to boil, she remembered how off-handedly her father had dismissed the idea of him planting a bug in the cabin. Sure, Axel's scenario was probably right. But if Lester Garrison and Daddy were in cahoots, there was no telling how far they'd go. Of course, they wouldn't be snooping for info about each other. Instead, they'd be keeping tabs on how well their little plan for Taylor and Axel went.

She frowned for a moment, then stuck her head out the door. "Axel! Have your cousins been up to see your cabin?"

He hollered back, "Yes, they have! Three times! Trying to talk me into selling the land to them."

There it was, the link she'd been looking for. Lester had only to send his nephews out to the cabin and get them to install some kind of bug. Maybe a tiny microphone, or even a hidden camera. She began searching for a device planted in the cabin. She peered under every shelf and counter. She moved the contents of the cupboards around, checking for a false container. She didn't bother to look in the corner where the Murphy bed was folded away. It was too far away from their work area. Besides, the only thing her father would have overheard there was Axel snoring at night, if he snored, that is.

Frustration set in as the tea kettle whistled. She took it off the stove and poured water over the tea bags in their mugs. While they steeped, she walked to the window to check on Axel's progress. He wasn't visible, but the large gathering of reindeer on the far side of the barn gave away his location. She still had time. She hadn't checked the light fixture yet. There was only one, above the table where they worked. She climbed onto a chair, but her five feet were insufficient to reach the light. So she stepped gingerly up onto the table.

She almost tumbled off when her foot landed on a stack of papers and they slid from under her. She caught her balance and calmed herself. At last she was tall enough to reach the light. It was a cheap domed fixture. She felt above her head for the screws holding the opaque dome to the frame.

"Lefty loosey," she mumbled to herself, as she turned each of the three screws just enough to let the dome slip out in her hand. She examined it closely, but there was nothing inside it. Besides, even a tiny microphone would have been visible as a shadow. She'd have to get a little closer to see if something was stuck up inside the fixture. She puzzled over her situation for a moment, then decided she could stack the two reams of printer paper and stand on those. That would elevate her another four or five inches. Just enough to get a better look.

She used the toes of her hiking boots to push one ream into place and she cringed at the chunks of corral mud that scattered on the table. She bent carefully to place the second ream on top of the first. Then she stepped up onto the stacked packages and squinted up at the lightbulb. Was it possible to hide something under the bulb? She took hold of it and unscrewed it, her attention focused on the dark interior of the fixture.

Axel entered the cabin along with a gust of brisk April air. It caught the door and slammed it open against the wood box. "What are you doing?!"

Taylor shrieked and lost her footing.

Axel lunged to keep her from falling off the table. Taylor grabbed at the nearest handhold which turned out to be Axel's hair.

"Ow!" He caught her around the waist as she fell sideways, and they both went down.

They froze. Axel couldn't move because her derriere had landed on his bread basket, and Taylor was mortified at being caught in the act of snooping in the cabin.

When Axel could breathe again, he nudged her gently off and rolled onto his knees. "That's the second time I've had to rescue you, girl. What in the world were you doing up on the table?"

Taylor stood and held up the light bulb. "I was checking to see if our fathers had somehow planted a listening device in your cabin."

"Oh, that's why you wanted to know if my cousins had been out here." Axel cocked his head to one side. "You think our fathers would stoop to snooping on the progress of our friendship?"

Taylor felt a twinge of disappointment. "Oh, our friendship. Goodness knows, I lip-lock with everyone I call a friend. You should see the lipstick smears on my computer screen from kissing all my Facebook friends." She tossed the lightbulb at him.

Axel caught the bulb and raised a dubious brow. "I was just being cautious," he said. "I didn't want to assume too much. Although I admit, considering the heat we were generating in the barn, I think we've escalated way beyond friendship." He shook the bulb next to his ear. "It sounds okay. Might as well change it as long as it's unscrewed." He started opening cupboards, and after a few moments, he looked at her curiously. "I take it you already looked in here?"

Taylor blushed. "Yes. I told you, I was looking for something hidden."

Axel humphed. "Self-sufficient. Like climbing on the table instead of waiting for me to return." He opened a lower cupboard and found a package of bulbs. "Here we go. Let me do the honors, okay?" He stepped up on a chair and screwed in the new bulb. Then he let Taylor hand him the dome so he could screw that on as well.

"There. All done. Is that my tea?"

"Yes. I made tea. Just like I said I would." She handed him his mug, still a bit hurt. She used the side of her hand to sweep little chunks of mud off the table into her other palm. "I should have waited for you. I apologize. I'm just used to handling things myself. So you don't think they want to spy on us?"

"Actually," whispered Axel, stepping closer, "I think you might be right. Except, in a manner we would never suspect." He put a finger to his lips, picked up her jacket, and lifted her purse from the floor to the table.

Chapter Twenty-Three

AXEL'S EYEBROWS ROSE IN A silent question and Taylor nodded her assent. Slowly, he opened her bag, and silently, item by item, they emptied its contents.

Wallet, change purse, keys, phone, lip gloss, compact, comb, three packs of Juicy Fruit gum, a small LED flashlight, a tin of Tylenol, a thumb drive, a pink plastic case, and a photograph of Taylor sitting proudly on a magnificent horse.

Axel whispered, "Is that Jackson?"

Taylor nodded and smiled.

Axel cleared his throat. "Okay, let's sit down and read over your notes," he said in a normal voice, motioning for Taylor to have a seat. "This biography isn't going to write itself."

Taylor frowned in confusion, then caught on. "Oh. Right you are. Let's get busy."

They sat down and silently examined each of the objects from her purse, looking for anything out of the ordinary. When Axel picked up the plastic case and started to open it, Taylor grabbed it out of his hands and checked it herself, half hidden under the table.

Axel whispered, "What is that?"

"Something you'll never need," she whispered back, replacing it in her purse.

After several minutes, they had to agree that nothing looked suspicious. Axel shook his head in frustration. He ran his hands over the bag. The leather was creamy and soft, and he was sure it cost at least as much as the blouse he'd replaced. The zipper closure moved smoothly to and fro. As he zipped it closed one last time, his fingers lingered on what appeared to be a white plastic square with a hole in one corner fastened to the zipper pull with a loop of wire. His brows knit together as he examined it.

Taylor started to speak. "Oh, that? It's—"

Axel pressed a finger to his lips and was pleased when Taylor fell silent. He pulled a piece of paper from the open ream on the table and handed her a pen. She scribbled a few words.

He read, *It's one of those chips that lets you find something you've lost.*

That seemed sensible. Axel flipped the device over and over in his fingers. Odd. It had tiny pinholes in it. He took the pen and wrote, *Have you ever used it?*

Taylor wrote back, *No. But Daddy thought it would be a good idea.*

Their eyes met, and Taylor's mouth dropped open.

Axel cautioned her again to be quiet. He wrote another line.

Test the program on your computer.

Taylor pulled the laptop out of its case and opened it up. A few seconds later, she found the app and activated it. She clicked on the "find" button. A small box appeared on the screen with the message, "No device detected."

Axel closed his fist around the white square before speaking. "Son of a gun. He put a listening device on your purse." He used his free hand to detach the wire loop from the zipper pull.

"But why? I already call him every night. Why would he need to listen in?"

"Because, silly girl, he doesn't trust you to tell him everything. At least now we know how he found out about us shipping Jackson to Colorado." He rubbed his chin. "Think back. Besides my father, what else have we talked about?"

"Well, it had to happen when my purse was around, so it was mostly what we talked about here. Nothing in the barn."

"That's a relief," said Axel.

"Most of what you said about your dad was positive anyway. And if they're working on some project together, he doesn't really need that kind of information. Do you think he's trying to pull a fast one on your father?"

Axel shook his head. "That's not an easy thing to do. My old man is a business genius, and he's got a very crafty head on his shoulders. I think they're working on something together, but if it's not getting the two of us together, what is it? And why would having a listening device on your purse help them with that?" He squeezed his fist tighter around the plastic square.

Taylor's eyes widened. "Maybe it's not a listening device. Maybe it's a tracking device!"

"Why would he put a tracking device on your purse?"

"When I was in college, some girlfriends and I decided to do Spring Break. We took off for Florida, just the four of us. No worries in the world. Had a great time that first night, partied until dawn. We danced and flirted with a bunch of guys. My roommate entered a wet tee-shirt contest. We had a ball.

"My friends got so wasted, they could barely walk back to the hotel. That's why I don't drink much. If I hadn't stayed sober that night, who knows what might have happened? When we finally got to our room, there were three burly guys waiting for us. For *me*. They'd tracked me down on my father's orders. They used the 'safe' word my parents had arranged for us as kids so I'd know they were legitimate. Then they basically said if I didn't go with them quietly, they would take me home by force."

Axel was stunned. "They got away with that? Didn't you press charges?"

"No, of course not." She looked horrified. "Against my father? They were working for him. He told me I'd made a horrible mistake by just taking off, and he never wanted me to do that again. One of his partners' kids had been snatched and held for ransom on a vacation to Mexico. I was only in Florida, but it freaked him out. Humiliated me. None of the girls ever invited me along again. I never figured out how they tracked me. I had turned off my phone, and we used cash instead of credit cards."

Axel wiggled the fist holding the plastic square. "I'll bet you took your purse."

Taylor sagged in her chair. "It was a different bag, but it had one of those tags on it."

Axel grinned. "With technology what it is today, it could be both a tracking device and a listening device." He thought for a moment. "I think I have an idea." He got up and pulled open a drawer beside the sink, then the one under that. "Here it is." He held up a five-by-eight-inch padded mailer and dropped the plastic square inside it. Then he sealed it up. "If it's a listening device, he won't hear much in there. And if it's a tracking device, well, he's going to track you to Las Vegas. That's where my cousin Uly and his wife, Belle, are staying at the moment. They're taking care of our godmother, Lulamae. She had a hip replaced." He wrote the address out by memory. "We'll drop it in the mail when I take you back into town. What time is it?"

"Almost one."

"We've got lots of time before Jackson arrives. I've been trying to figure out what else our fathers are up to. And I think we should go have a talk with Lucy Baxter."

Chapter Twenty-Four

TAYLOR KNEW IT WAS SILLY to want to stay and wait at the cabin when Jackson wouldn't be delivered until four. Her latest cell phone update had told her the flying stable had just landed in Denver. They still had to transfer him to a horse trailer and drive him to Axel's place. So she didn't object to Axel's plan to talk to Lucy. How could she refuse him anything after he'd arranged to bring her horse to Colorado? Besides, she was burning with curiosity to know what their fathers were up to.

Axel's property had been part of the Lazy B, so they weren't far away from Lucy's ranch house as the crow flies, but driving there took them twenty minutes. Lucy was in front of the rambling house, and since it was still April, there were only a handful of guests scattered about the area. Most were hanging out by the corral, watching a little girl take a riding lesson.

Lucy greeted them before they even got out of the SUV. "Axel Garrison, as I live and breathe! What can I do for you today?" Her smile was as bright as the midday sun.

Axel and Taylor got out and they each shook Lucy's hand. Axel said, "You remember Taylor?"

"Of course. And the way she took charge of Thunder? You betcha."

Taylor was pleased. It was always fun to get a compliment for her riding skills. "Thanks, Lucy."

Axel said, "Her warmblood, Jackson, is arriving later this afternoon. You'll have a chance to meet him soon."

Lucy's eyes lit up and she canted a brow. "Moving your horse out to Colorado? Do I sense a budding romance?"

Taylor blushed hotly and looked away.

Lucy laughed sweetly. "I'll shut up," she said. "Didn't mean to embarrass you. But you probably didn't drive over here to tell me about your horse." She looked questioningly from one to the other.

Axel rubbed his chin. "Actually, I was wondering if we could ask you a few questions about the property sale."

"Y'all find a problem?" She looked worried.

"Not at all," Axel reassured her. "You know I'm in love with the place. But when you originally showed me the property, you mentioned that a couple of unofficial offers had come in before I showed up and how they had you worried. Do you still have those around?"

"Sure do. Come on in, we'll get some coffee."

They followed her into the house.

Taylor said, "This is lovely! Look at that fireplace. So rustic and charming. Axel says the Lazy B is a dude ranch now. I imagine you must do a brisk business."

"Mostly in the summer," she said. "But yeah, I had to get inventive to save the place. Long story. Short version—a banker refused me a loan a couple of years ago, and I needed cash in a hurry. I never thought I'd enjoy being a western guest ranch, but…" She lowered her voice and leaned toward them. "…I'm starting to love it."

They were in the kitchen now, where three cooks were hard at work. One was pulling a large tray of cookies out of the oven.

Taylor took a deep breath. "Oh, chocolate chip! My favorite," she sighed.

"Then we'll have a few," said Lucy. She spoke to the rotund woman with the spatula in her hand. "We'll have three coffees, too." Then to Axel and Taylor, "Y'all sit down. I'll go fetch them papers."

Taylor looked around with an appreciative eye. "This kitchen means business," she said. "It looks like Lucy is quite the entrepreneur." She smiled at the cook who was setting mugs and a plate of warm cookies on the table. "How many guests to do you have at peak season?"

The woman's ruddy cheeks lifted in a smile. She said, "We have five bedrooms in the house and we've added a cabin with four guest rooms, so that's nine all together, and people often share, so we had anywhere from eighteen to twenty-four guests at a time last season. This year, we're booking more and racing to finish another four-suite cabin before June first."

Axel teased, "No wonder things have slowed down on my house construction. Everyone in the area is over here building cabins."

Lucy arrived in time to hear his comment. She laughed. "Sorry about that, Axel." She set three letters on the table. "These are what you were asking about."

Taylor was surprised. "Letters? I thought we'd be looking at email printouts. Who sends letters these days?"

Lucy shrugged. "Seemed normal enough to me, but I'm old enough to remember when letters were the norm." She sat down and doctored her coffee with sugar and cream. "Help yourself to cookies."

"Thanks," said Taylor. She lifted a warm cookie and inhaled its fragrance. "Heavenly."

Lucy grinned.

Axel began examining the letters. "This one makes sense," he said, showing Taylor the envelope. It had come from Thor Garrison and bore the return address of Thor Security. "My cousin was so mad at me for buying the place at the asking price. Look, Taylor. He's telling Lucy she'll never sell the property for that much money."

Taylor nodded. "Looks like he was trying to manipulate the asking price without actually submitting an official low bid." She bit into her cookie and moaned with pleasure.

"Here's another," said Axel, "and a third, but these are from people I never heard of." He frowned at the signature on one of the letters. "I could swear that handwriting looks familiar."

Taylor leaned toward him to examine the letter he was staring at. It had a return address from Pawling, New York. She swallowed a bite of cookie, then asked, "Didn't you go to school in Pawling?"

Axel frowned at the return address. "Yes." He looked at the signature again. "For Pete's sake! I could swear this is my father's handwriting."

Taylor examined the third letter. "One East 161st Street, The Bronx, New York." She squeezed Axel's arm. "This return address is totally bogus. That's Yankee Stadium!"

Lucy looked puzzled. "What on Earth? Who would do that?"

Taylor examined the signature on the Yankee Stadium letter, then gawked. "The handwriting on this one looks familiar, too. I think our fathers have a lot of explaining to do."

Chapter Twenty-Five

AXEL SHOOK HIS HEAD OVER the letters. "Lucy, it's beginning to look like my father and Taylor's father were joining forces with Thor to convince you to lower your price. And from what these letters say, I'm ashamed to admit they were practically trying to steal it."

"The price I asked you for had already come down a hundred thousand from the original," said Lucy. "Boy, was I ever glad to have you move to Eagle's Toe."

"It was a fair price," said Axel. "And worth every penny. I plan to be there a long time. Once your cabins are completed, my new house should go up fairly quickly. I'm going for the log cabin look, so it'll blend well with the trees and the bass lake. I hope to move into the first stage before next winter."

Taylor perked up. "Who's your designer?"

Axel looked left, then right, searching for an answer.

Taylor sighed. "Interior designer? Please don't tell me you expect it to look like the cabin you're in now." There was a hint of playfulness to her tone.

Axel was embarrassed to admit it, but he hadn't given a thought to the interior. "I may need some help in that area," he confessed. Then he placed his hand over hers. "Any suggestions?"

Taylor tilted her head to one side. "I may have an idea or two."

Lucy chuckled. "Sounds like letting Taylor take charge of the interior is a good idea. Oh, excuse me. I hear a truck on the gravel. The mail is here."

"We'll walk out with you," said Axel. "I've got an envelope in the car that I'd like to send on its way as soon as possible."

After handing the mailer over to the postman, Axel and Taylor headed back to the cabin.

At four p.m., a large red pickup and horse trailer pulled up in front of the barn.

Taylor was beside herself with joy. Two men alighted from the pickup. One had paperwork for Axel, and the other trotted to the back of the horse trailer to open the door. Jackson nickered a soft greeting from inside.

Two hours later, after walking Jackson around the barn and corrals, letting him meet the reindeer and catch the scent of alpacas on the wind, they got him settled in his new stall.

Axel leaned against the stall door, propping his chin on his arms. "I think your horse is very fond of Rita the Reindeer."

"Rita? I'd have thought you'd pick more traditional names, like Prancer and Dancer."

"Oh, those particular reindeer still live at the Lazy B. I have the breeding stock over here. Did you know that female reindeer keep their horns all through the winter? The males shed theirs long before Christmas. So all of Santa's reindeer are ladies."

Taylor smiled. "That makes a lot of sense, actually." She stroked Jackson's forehead as he nuzzled the pockets of her jacket for treats.

Axel smiled back. "Jackson is very happy to see you."

"Thank you so much for bringing him to Eagle's Toe." She turned her big blue eyes in Axel's direction.

He sidled closer, laying a hand on Jackson's neck as he did so. "My mother loved horses so much," he said.

"Maybe it's time for you to add to your stable," said Taylor. "I mean, what is money for if you can't indulge in what you love? You're doing great rescue work here, but you could honor your mother's passion for horses by taking in a few rescued equines."

Axel considered the suggestion. "That's a great idea. I hadn't thought of that." He patted Jackson's neck, and the horse responded by nibbling at his arm. "I don't understand how your father can resent the time you spend with this magnificent animal."

Taylor slipped an arm around Axel's waist. "Jackson likes you. He's a very good judge of character. You just scored a bazillion points."

Axel grinned. "Glad to hear it." He pulled her closer with one arm.

Taylor said, "I tried to please Daddy every way I could. I majored in business at school. I showed as much interest in the family companies as he would let me. I mean, insurance? Finance? Stocks and bonds?" She shrugged. "Why can't we do something hands on, something that's more than numbers on a computer screen?"

Axel fed Jackson a sugar cube. "I think you'd make a great businesswoman," he said, "in the right field. How do you feel about retail? Mr. Parker is getting ready to retire, and his kids have scattered to do other things. Eagle's Toe will always need a feed and grain store."

Taylor's expression turned thoughtful. "That's not a bad idea." Her tone brightened. "I could spend my days surrounded by saddles and bridles instead of slogging around the company mailroom!"

"Sounds like you and your father have very different ideas about the path to happiness."

Taylor leaned her head against his shoulder. "Sort of like you and your dad."

"Really?"

"You don't seem to have much in common either. He's a billionaire businessman, and you are a talented novelist who wants to rescue animals. He's a ruthless negotiator, and you are a gentle soul." She paused before adding, "I think I would have really liked your mother. I'll bet you're just like her." Then she turned away to press her face against Jackson's cheek, afraid she'd revealed too much.

Axel searched for something to say. "So, shall I drive you back to the hotel, or did you want to sleep in the barn with Jackson?"

"Don't tempt me!" Taylor looked up at him, love in her eyes. "We need to get you a horse," she murmured.

"Why, Miss Hazen, that is the sexiest thing anyone ever said to me." Axel bent to kiss her softly on the lips.

Jackson shoved Axel with his head.

Taylor laughed. "Okay, okay, Jackson. You're right." Her voice softened. "Staying here would be a very dangerous idea."

Axel held her gaze for several long seconds before forcing himself to look away. "I'll wait for you in the car."

"I'll get my computer." She headed for the cabin.

When she got there, she could hear her phone ringing in her purse. She pulled it out, heaved a sigh, and answered the call.

"Hello, Daddy."

"Where the hell have you been?!"

Chapter Twenty-Six

TAYLOR WAS TAKEN ABACK. "What do you mean?"

"I haven't heard from you in—" He broke off.

Taylor propped one hand on her hip. "In what? Twenty-two hours? I just called you last night."

Silence.

Then, "Well, be sure to call me again tonight. I told you, I need that info by Friday!" And he hung up.

Taylor stared at her phone, shaking her head. She gathered her computer and her purse and joined Axel at the SUV where she loaded her things into the cab and climbed in. "I just had the weirdest call from my father."

"What'd he say?" Axel got behind the wheel.

"He was angry that he hadn't heard from me since last night." She clicked her seat belt into place.

Axel laughed. "Well, at least we know that the little plastic square was definitely a listening device."

Taylor's eyes widened. "Oh my gosh, that's what he meant! He stopped himself, too, before he could say how long it had been since he heard from me."

Axel started the car and headed down his dirt road. "I'll bet it's been…" He glanced at the dash clock. "…at least five hours. That's how long ago we popped that thing in the envelope."

Taylor laughed. "It's a relief to know he can't eavesdrop on every word." She shook her head. "I'm so angry with him. He really doesn't trust me at all. I'm just a chess piece in some bigger game he's playing."

"Don't take it too hard," said Axel. "You're not in this alone."

Taylor smiled, then ducked her head to keep from showing her pleasure at his words. "What do you think they're really up to?" she asked.

Axel shook his head. "Not sure. We know they were helping Thor try to bring the price down on the property. That makes sense if Thor wants to build housing on it, because a development like that is a huge investment. But considering the amount of money floating around between your family and mine, if they were ready to buy, the asking price wouldn't have mattered. I mean, they could have done it easily. So why were they waiting?"

Taylor frowned. "Daddy loves it when he gets a bargain."

"I just think this is more than bargain hunting. They wanted the property for a reason, but I bought it before they could make their move. So far, they haven't made any real money offers to me, but I have received some pressure from my cousins. You know, asking me what the heck I'm doing, putting one house on a huge piece of acreage, living the country boy life. But they haven't really pushed hard about it."

Taylor stared out the window. "This is such beautiful country. I think you made the right decision. Keep it pristine. Or almost pristine. An animal sanctuary is a noble cause."

"Thanks." Axel reached out and took her hand. "It's such a puzzle though. I mean, should we still be working on this biography? Or was it all a sham to send you out here with that listening-slash-tracking device to eavesdrop on something other than our conversations?"

"Like what? We've spent all our time together."

"Not quite," said Axel. "You go back to the hotel every night. You went shoe shopping at Mina's Boutique, and I wasn't along for that."

"How do you know that's where I bought them?"

"Your rental car is in Brady's garage. No other place you could get to on foot from the Cattleman's. Besides, everyone shops at Mina's. So what did you two talk about?"

Taylor shrugged. "We talked about shoes, actually. And she told me a little about your cousin Thor and…oh! She mentioned that the town council had voted down fracking and oil stuff. I didn't know there was oil in Colorado."

"Seventh largest producer of crude in the U.S.," said Axel.

Taylor gawked at him. "How did you know that?"

"The Garrison money comes from oil. My uncle, Rudy, is still in the oil business." He hit the brakes and pulled the SUV onto the shoulder of the road. "Son of a gun! Could that be it? I left that meeting in the middle because I was tired of watching Thor trying to browbeat the council over zoning. They must have talked about fracking at the end."

"But why would your cousin want that kind of industry here when he's trying to convince the council to let him build luxury homes?"

Axel looked grim. "Maybe he doesn't know anything about it. I'll bet they're letting him think they're interested in his luxury homes idea. We need to talk to Thor."

Taylor touched his cheek and her fingers tingled with his energy. "But not tonight. Stay in town long enough to have dinner. No one can hear us talking now." She smiled flirtatiously and hefted her purse. "And I won't keep you too late. After all, my horse is in your barn."

"Just dinner, huh?" Axel's voice grew husky.

Taylor looked apologetic. "You're the one who said we have to wait because of your father's silly wedding toast."

Axel gazed softly into her eyes. "I guess the least I can do is have dinner. Like you said, your horse is in my barn. That counts for something."

"More than you know," said Taylor sweetly.

Axel rubbed a hand over his face, fending off the attraction between them. "Okay. Let's go eat. I'm starved."

Taylor laughed. "Gee, that was romantic."

When they got to the Cattleman's, Taylor said, "Let me run upstairs and change into something prettier."

Axel held his arms out. "Please don't make me feel like a plaid suit at a fancy ball."

Taylor paused, looking him up and down. She said softly, "I think you look great. Every inch the gentleman rancher. But I know what you mean." She lifted one mud-encrusted hiking boot in the air. "I'm just going to change my shoes and comb the hay out of my hair."

"I'll put our names on the reservation list," said Axel. He watched her move toward the elevators, computer bag over one arm, purse over the other, and marveled that she could make that look sexy. Especially considering the state of her hiking boots. Shaking his head in wonder, he approached the hostess at the Il Vaccaro Italian restaurant off the lobby and learned that they would only have to wait ten minutes for a table. He strolled to the historic photos on the wall and caught his reflection in one of them. Taylor wasn't the only one with hay in her hair!

He decided it was worth a stop at the men's room because the picture glass wasn't the best mirror. Besides, if he was going to have dinner with a fine-looking woman like Taylor, he wanted to measure up. It was already seven. His five-o'clock shadow was fashionable these days, so he didn't worry about that. But it did take him a few minutes to pick the hay and some unidentifiable bits of green out of his hair. At last, he broke down and paid a dollar for a comb out of a machine on the wall. When he viewed the result, he decided it was worth the money.

He returned to the lobby not a moment too soon. As he struck a casual pose near the restaurant entrance and turned to watch the comings and goings at registration, he spotted Taylor on her way over from the elevators. Her blue bob was flawless. And although she was still wearing jeans, she had changed into a demure white blouse with a ruched midriff and white heels. The sight of her caused his heart to skip a beat as he realized for the first time how hooked he was on Miss Taylor Hazen.

"Did I take too long?" she asked.

Unable to form words, Axel shook his head and waved an arm toward the restaurant. Curse his father's drunken wedding toast! How was he possibly going to stay away from Taylor long enough to ruin the old man's devious plans?

Chapter Twenty-Seven

Tuesday, April 12

TAYLOR DREAMED OF WEDDING GOWNS and horses. As she woke up, the last shreds of her dream fading, she could distinctly remember Jackson being their ring bearer. It was the image of her horse decked out in flowers, walking down the aisle of the church, that nudged her awake.

She luxuriated in the silken sheets of her bedroom suite and let herself relive the magical evening she'd shared with Axel. First, they had dinner at Il Vaccaro. Then they'd gone to a tiny restaurant up the street for dessert.

"What a perfect name for a tiny restaurant! The Itty Bitty."

Axel seemed to know everyone in town, and they were warmly welcomed and treated to tiramisu perfection by Alice Kate McAvoy, the owner. By nine-thirty, they were stuffed to the gills and holding hands like teenagers over their coffee. For several long minutes, they stared into each other's eyes.

At last, Axel spoke. "I hate to say it, but I have to get back to the cabin and check on the animals before bedtime."

"I know. Jackson loves those horse treats we bought at the Feed and Grain. Be sure to give him one when you say good-night."

Axel nodded. "I will." But neither of them moved an inch.

Alice Kate brought their bill. Axel glanced at it, then protested, "On the house? No way. You can't just give food away, Alice Kate. You'll go out of business."

Alice Kate winked. "I have a secret partner, a sugar daddy, so to speak. I was just talking to him a moment ago, and he said you'd spent a fortune on your dinner. So dessert is on me. You need more coffee." She patted Axel on the shoulder, then bustled off to her kitchen.

"Wow," said Taylor, "people here really love you."

Axel gave a tiny shrug, like it was no big deal. "I saved the Lazy B," he said. "I guess that made me a hero of sorts."

Alice Kate was back in time to overhear Axel's words. "Too bad you couldn't bail out the Pattersons," she said. "I heard a rumor today that they're thinking of selling out."

"Oh no," said Axel. "They have a huge place, too. Is someone local buying it?"

"Not sure, but rumor has it the offer came from back east somewhere."

Taylor said, "Maybe they want to keep it as a ranch, like Axel's doing."

"We can only hope," said Alice Kate before retreating again.

Axel frowned. "When we visit Thor tomorrow, I'll ask him if he's heard anything. Maybe after I bought the Lazy B parcel, he started looking around for a different piece of land."

"But she said the offer came from back east."

Axel raised a brow. "She said, 'rumor has it.' In my experience, that's not the most trustworthy source of information." He glanced at his phone. "I'd better get you back to the hotel. You can sleep in tomorrow. Thor doesn't open his doors until ten a.m. I'll meet you here and we'll walk up the street to his store."

"Thor Security?"

"That's it."

And that was why she was letting herself lie in bed like a woman of leisure. Axel wouldn't arrive until ten. After a few moments, she sighed dreamily. She reached for her phone and glanced at the screen.

"Nine-thirty-two?!" How could she have slept so long? She blamed it on the wedding dream. She threw off the covers and dashed for the shower. It's not that she was rushing things. No one had control over their dreams, did they? But she knew she'd fallen hard for Axel. Two weeks ago, she'd never heard of him. And here she was, head over heels.

But he loved her back. She just knew it. She couldn't wait to see him again, and help him figure out what their fathers were up to.

She took the fastest shower of her life, then selected her outfit at a saner pace. She decided to go casual. She wanted to look more like an

Eagle's Toe resident. She picked her plainest pair of designer jeans, a modest pale blue tee, and a sweater that matched her eyes and hair. She frowned at her blue tint. She needed a refresher. Maybe she'd ask at registration. Hadn't she seen a hair salon in the commercial wing off the lobby? Near that little coffee shop? She'd look later. She slipped her feet into a pair of Nikes. She'd left her galoshes in Axel's truck, so if things got muddy, she'd be okay.

She managed to pull herself together quickly enough to grab her purse and make it to the elevator by nine-fifty-five. She left her computer in her room. If they wound up actually continuing with this biographical ruse, she'd take notes by hand.

Axel was already in the lobby, waiting for her by the coffee and pastry table. She felt her heart race at the sight of him. Why hadn't she met him in New York? They both grew up there, and obviously their families were in the same financial class. How could they have missed each other?

She knew the answer immediately. He'd been at an all-boys prep school and they'd gone to different colleges. So it wasn't as if they'd been attending the same parties or anything. And besides, it didn't matter. She'd finally met him here, she'd fallen in love with him here, and she wanted to spend the rest of her days with him here. In Eagle's Toe, Colorado. Life was full of surprises.

When she approached, he bent to kiss her softly on the lips.

"I'm happy to report that a certain fussy warmblood is settling in well and Rita the Reindeer already thinks he's king of the barn."

"Wonderful!" That deserved another kiss.

"No computer?"

"We'll play it by ear. Why labor all day and find out it was all just make-work in the end?"

"Can't argue there. That means you can spend the afternoon riding Jackson."

Taylor squealed. She couldn't help herself. "Sorry," she said, "I'm just so excited to have him here."

"Breakfast?" Axel lifted an apple fritter. "These are from The Muffin Man."

"Oh, in that case…." She picked up a paper napkin and selected a twisted glazed donut. "This is so decadent." She filled a cup with coffee and snapped a plastic lid on it.

"I'm parked out front."

"I thought we were walking over to Thor Security?"

"Last night, Mrs. McAvoy said the Pattersons are getting ready to sell their place. I thought we'd drive out and talk to them first. Just a hunch."

"Okay." The Pattersons' name sparked a memory. "Mina also mentioned the Shanes were having financial problems. Is that important?"

"Could be. We'll stop there first."

Taylor didn't know exactly what kind of information Axel thought he could get from two local ranchers, especially ones who weren't doing well financially, but she was with Axel and she wasn't staring at a computer screen, so she decided to relax and enjoy herself.

When Axel pulled onto Highway 50 eastbound, Taylor said, "I've never been this way before."

"The Patterson place and the Shane ranch are both east of town," he said. "It won't take long on the highway."

Taylor didn't mind. She munched on her donut and sipped her coffee. The farther east they went, the more pastureland they saw. The number of trees lessened, and instead of evergreens, she spotted large gatherings of aspen, their spring green leaves trembling in the breeze over strikingly white trunks. It looked like they were murmuring secrets to each other in the morning air.

They passed fields filled with cattle on one side of the highway and sheep on the other side. Two border collies were intent on taking their flock away from the road and were doing an efficient job of it. A fence separated the field from the road, but the dogs weren't about to trust their charges to wood and wire. Taylor wondered if she and Axel should get a border collie. He could get lots of exercise herding those stinking alpacas.

When Axel slowed to make a left turn onto a gravel road, he paused long enough to let a BMW pull out onto the highway, headed west.

"Who's that?" asked Taylor.

"I'm not sure," said Axel. He sniffed the air. "Smells like a lawyer."

Taylor laughed. "Most of the lawyers I know prowl around the big city. What's one doing at the Shanes' place?"

"Let's go find out."

Chapter Twenty-Eight

AXEL DROVE SLOWLY TOWARD THE FARM house. It looked in need of a coat of paint. It was supposed to be white, but there were so many strips of peeling paint, it almost resembled the bark of the aspens that shaded it. A beat up old flatbed was parked off to the side with six bales of hay on the back.

Standing in front of the porch, wringing her hands, was a middle-aged woman wearing jeans and a barn coat. Wisps of greying hair escaped from under her battered Stetson. As they pulled up, Axel realized she was wiping her fingers on a handkerchief. He parked behind the flatbed and got out, coming around to open Taylor's door for her.

"Morning, Mrs. Shane," he said pleasantly. "I think we met last week at a city council meeting. Or was it the Grange lodge?"

Mrs. Shane's brown eyes were sharp and observant. Axel let her take him in from head to toe while he offered Taylor a hand as she stepped out of the SUV.

Mrs. Shane's voice was calm and measured. "The Grange," she said. "I remember you. You're cousin to the Garrison boys."

"That's right." Axel smiled. "This is my friend, Taylor."

"Oh yeah, the new girl from back east. Mina told me." She held out a hand. "Nice to meet you, Taylor. I'm Marigold." She glanced from Taylor to Axel and back again as she shook Taylor's hand. "Has he asked you yet?"

Taylor blushed. "Um, no. I mean, asked me? I mean…."

Marigold laughed and released her hand. "I'm just teasing. You make a nice couple, that's all. What can I do for you, Axel?"

Axel indicated the hanky in her hand. "Did you touch something?"

"Yeah. Shook a lawyer's hand. Trying to get the stink off."

Axel chuckled. "His car looked familiar."

"He was at the Grange meeting, too. Works for one of the Garrisons."

Axel's brows rose. "Oh, right. I remember now."

Marigold stuffed the hanky in her coat pocket. "It's nice to see you and all, but I'm in the middle of chores. What can I do you for?"

Axel loved the way his neighbors talked. He tilted his head to one side. "Well, you know I bought a parcel from the Lazy B."

"Yep. Your cousin Thor was none too pleased, as I recall."

"You might say that. Yesterday, I was talking to Mrs. Baxter, and she told me she'd received some letters trying to pressure her into lowering her price before I came along. I was wondering if anyone had been out here trying to buy your place?"

Marigold stared at him for several seconds. Then she said, "Chores can wait. Come inside and set a spell. Got something to show you."

The outside of the house may have needed painting, but the inside was a cozy showcase. Overstuffed chairs, throw rugs on the burnished wooden floors, a fat black wood stove standing where a fireplace used to be. The mantle remained, covered with photos of different sizes, and on the walls were more pictures, boys and girls with big blue and red ribbons, standing next to pigs and sheep and goats.

"Come on into the kitchen," said Marigold. She waved a hand at the photos as if they were nothing, but there was pride in her voice. "All my kids did Four-H. Always came home with ribbons."

The kitchen was warm and smelled of fresh-baked bread. Next to a modern electric stove stood an old-fashioned cast iron monster. "That was my grandmother's cook stove," said Marigold. "Never could bring myself to get rid of it. And it still comes in handy, too. Makes the best bread ever. Have a seat. My husband's in the barn. One of our pigs is in labor." She set a bread board on the table and cut four slices off the end. "Just took it out of the oven half an hour ago. Help yourselves." She took the glass top off the butter dish and pulled a knife out of a drawer. "Coffee?"

Taylor started to object, but Axel responded first. "Coffee would be lovely, if it's not too much trouble."

"No trouble at all, just made a fresh pot."

Once they were settled and had a chance to taste the homemade bread, Axel said, "Mmmm, this bread is amazing!"

Marigold was pleased. "Thank you. Been making my own since I was thirteen." She pulled open a drawer on her side of the table and lifted a handful of papers out. "Here's what I wanted to show you."

Axel took another bite of the heavenly bread, then pulled the papers close enough to read. There were five letters and several brochures about fracking and how it would make the Shanes a ton of money.

Marigold said, "That lawyer brought those pamphlets to the Grange that night. Guess he thought we were ready to take the bait. He was out here this morning talking a mile a minute about all the opportunities he was ready to hand us on a silver platter."

Axel perused the letters. He spotted a familiar return address and tapped a finger on it. "Gee, someone must have rented office space at Yankee Stadium."

Taylor barked a laugh. "Right. Like that would ever happen. Do you recognize the signature?"

"Well, the name is bogus, I'm sure, but I don't think it's my father's handwriting. What about you?"

Taylor shook her head. "Never saw it before."

"But this one looks familiar, doesn't it?" He picked up a letter with a Pawling return address and passed it to Taylor.

"That's the same name he used on the Lazy B letter."

Marigold looked from one to the other. "My husband and I were thinking about selling. We had a hard couple of years, and there's things that need doing that we can't quite afford. We was tempted."

Axel looked at her anxiously. "Tempted?"

Marigold shrugged. "I just couldn't stand the idea of having all that oil business and all that equipment and everything on my property. They kept talking like we'd still own everything and they were just leasing, but I don't know." She shook her head. "There was something about it I just didn't trust. And like my husband says, if you smell dead fish, watch out for the bear."

Axel said, "Mrs. Shane, would you mind holding onto these letters for a while? Lucy Baxter got some from the same people. I thought my cousin was trying to get my eighty acres so he could build houses, but after looking at these, I'm not so sure it's that cut and dried. Did you get any offers or communications from Thor Garrison?"

"Nope. I might have paid attention to that. Just the ones you see here."

"If you don't mind me asking," said Axel, "are you having a better year?"

Marigold looked pleased. "My daughter was horrified that we might sell the family ranch, so she put her house in Denver on the market, and she's coming home to help us out. Says she wants to raise her kids here. She's still single at the moment, but wouldn't it be great to have grandkids running around the place?"

"That's fantastic," said Axel. "Well, we'd better get going. I want to stop by the Patterson place."

Marigold's expression darkened. "Their kids wouldn't come home to help on a bet. But don't tell Doreen I said that. Just give her my love." She stood up and pulled a large paper bag out of a drawer, took her other loaf of fresh bread, and put it in the bag. "And give her this. And tell her to call me. My chickens are pumping out eggs like crazy. I got lots to share."

Back in the SUV, Axel let Taylor hold the bread. "Sounds like the Pattersons aren't doing quite as well as the Shanes," he said.

Taylor looked at him, her brow furrowed with worry. "I can't stand the thought of this beautiful countryside having oil rigs all over it."

Axel looked grim. "Let's go see if the Pattersons have done something desperate."

Chapter Twenty-Nine

THE PATTERSON PLACE WAS ON THE other side of the highway a few miles further on. No BMW pulled out in front of them as they turned south onto yet another gravel road, but that didn't mean the Pattersons hadn't received a visit. The house was hidden behind a copse of aging oak trees. The barn came into view first, and it looked dilapidated. Almost all the paint had faded, and the wood underneath had weathered to a silver gray. When Axel turned onto the drive in front of the house itself, Taylor was saddened to see that it wasn't much better off than the barn. But floral curtains fluttered in the windows, and three overfed dogs announced their arrival as they clambered off the porch toward the SUV.

"Don't hit the dogs," said Taylor.

Axel smiled. "I won't. Doesn't look like they've missed a meal, does it?"

"Those aren't border collies."

"No, they're Australian shepherds, but it looks like their herding days are behind them. Good watch dogs though." He turned off the engine and got out of the car, then opened Taylor's door for her. As she stepped down, he spoke to the dogs. "Hey, guys, how's it going?"

His soothing voice stopped the barking and started the tail wagging, but their tails were only a couple of inches long, so they twisted their butts in his direction to let him know they were happy to see him.

Taylor was impressed. "Gee, you just have a knack with all animals, don't you?" She assured herself that adding dogs to Axel's collection would not be hard.

A worried-looking woman in faded jeans and a hand-me-down flannel shirt opened the screen door to quiet the dogs. "Hush now! You did your job. Get up here on the porch." The dogs obeyed. The woman squinted at them.

Axel spoke up before approaching the porch. "Mrs. Patterson? I'm Axel Garrison. We met at the Grange a while back."

Her expression eased. "Oh hello! Come on in. My husband is in the kitchen, working."

Carrying the bread bag, Taylor followed Axel into the house. Even though the outside was in desperate need of attention, it was obvious that Mrs. Patterson tried hard to keep the inside neat and tidy. But the furniture was old, and years of back and forth had worn a path in the green carpet. A television sat in the corner tuned to CNN, but the sound was off.

Mrs. Patterson led the way into the kitchen, where a sixty-something man sat in a wheelchair at the table. It was covered with pieces of leather in all states of being worked. Against the wall to his left was a special sewing machine with what looked like the handle of a handbag under the foot. He was rubbing emollient into a horse halter. Several finished pieces hung from the wall and waited for their turn on the table.

Taylor's eyes widened as she took it all in. She handed the bread bag to Mrs. Patterson. "Mrs. Shane sends her love and wanted you to have this fresh bread. Oh my goodness, Mr. Patterson, did you make all this?"

Mr. Patterson paused and looked up at the visitors. "Got more in the dining room. Getting ready for a big craft fair in Pueblo next week. Name's Andy. Who are you?" He spoke like a man of few words who didn't want to waste any on personal pronouns.

"I'm Taylor Hazen."

Axel spoke up. "Andy, good to see you again." They shook hands.

"Morning, Axel. Was pleased by your little talk at the Grange." His pale blue eyes were keen and his hands were steady, but only his bony knees supported the stained khaki trousers he wore. His eyes went back and forth between Axel and Taylor. "This your fiancée?" One corner of his mouth quirked up in a smile.

Axel cleared his throat and stumbled over his response. "Yes. No. Not officially."

Taylor let her mouth fall open as if she were surprised to hear how he felt. "Axel Garrison, I heard that. You said yes first. And you did it in front of witnesses." She grabbed his hand and grinned at him.

Andy laughed out loud. "Doreen, cut into that bread. Have a seat, you two. We don't get many visitors. We got coffee."

Axel pulled out a chair for Taylor, then sat next to her. "Thanks, Andy. Coffee would be great."

Doreen nodded and began fussing with mugs and a bread knife.

Taylor added, "Oh, I just remembered, Mrs. Shane says she has a surplus of eggs and would love to share. She wants you to call her."

Doreen's cheeks colored a bit. "That's awful nice of her. I'll do that." She kept her back to them.

Andy set the halter aside. "Got horses?" He directed the question to Taylor.

"Yes. I have a warmblood named Jackson, and that halter would look so good on him."

"Lots of tack in the dining room. Got to work fast before the craft fair."

"Are you selling at horse shows?"

"Well, I would, but you can't do every show, you know."

Doreen added, "Their entry fees run to the hundreds."

Andy pretended he didn't hear her. "I know you didn't come out here to talk leatherworking. What's up?"

Axel accepted a mug of coffee from Doreen as he explained. "We heard a rumor that you were thinking of selling the place."

"Nope. Gonna die here."

"Well, that's a relief." Axel stuttered to clarify as Andy stared in reproach. "I mean, I'm so glad you're not selling. But I was wondering if you had any offers? The reason I'm asking, Mrs. Baxter and the Shanes have received very similar letters urging them to either sell cheap or to lease to the oil people."

"Fracking." Andy spat the word.

Doreen set a plate of sliced bread on the table. "It could pay a lot of bills," she said in a tone that told Taylor she and her husband had been talking about the idea for quite a while.

"We'd have no room for livestock."

Doreen looked sad. "We ain't had any since the accident. Why do you keep hoping that will change?"

Andy smacked the table with one hand. "Because it's what we've done all our lives!" He looked away, struggling to control his anger.

Axel stared into his coffee for a few seconds. "Sorry to bring up such a sore subject," he said softly. "I just wanted to let you know that there may be other options."

"Don't go getting his hopes up," said Doreen. "This ain't been easy."

Taylor raised a timid hand. "May I ask what happened?"

Andy sighed. "I got kicked by a bull. Broke my pelvis. End of story."

Taylor squeezed Axel's arm. "There must be something we can do to help."

Doreen straightened her spine. "Maybe you'd like to see what we're selling in Pueblo."

"I'd love to," said Taylor. She got up and followed Doreen out of the room. Behind her, she could hear Axel's voice, talking earnestly with Andy. Then she saw the hundreds of items of handworked leather and gasped. "Oh my, these are stunning!" She moved through the room as if it were a sacred place. "These are for sale?"

Doreen allowed that they were. "I been putting price tags on everything, getting ready to load the truck next week."

"Do you have to do all the set up by yourselves?"

"At the craft show? Folks are really helpful, and they knew Andy before the accident, so they pitch in and give us a hand."

"I'm so glad. Wow. He really should be selling at every horse show he can. These bridles and martingales are spectacular!"

"He can do a special order for you after the craft show. You said your horse's name is Jackson? He could put Jackson's name on the cheek strap of a bridle or whatever you want."

Taylor was practically jumping up and down. Then she had an idea. "How much do you need for the entry fee to sell at a horse show?"

"The one coming up in Pueblo next month? They want three hundred dollars up front. Craft show's only a hundred."

Taylor ran her hands over a leather handbag with a horse's head stamped in the center of the design. "I really want this bag. And those two small matching shoulder bags, too. The ones with horseshoes on them. I need those for gifts." She moved through the room, making her selections. By the time she finished, she'd spent six hundred dollars. She pulled out her wallet and took six of the hundred-dollar bills that Axel had given her to replace her Armani blouse. "Here you go. Now please, see if you can get a space to sell at that horse show, because your husband is an artist and horse people will be fighting over these things."

Doreen looked overcome. "Do you really think so?"

"I'm sure of it! Wait until I tell Karla. I'm going to give her and her friend Mindy these shoulder bags. I'll tell her about special orders, too."

A moment later, Taylor had the wind squished out of her as Doreen gave her a powerful hug.

"Thank you," she babbled. "Thank you, thank you."

Once the hug ended, Taylor said, "You're very welcome. Do you sell online?"

Doreen's eyes glazed over.

"No," said Taylor, "I don't suppose you do. We'll talk about that another day."

"I've got to show Andy," said Doreen, waving the six crisp bills in the air.

She headed for the kitchen and Taylor followed, her arms filled with her purchases.

Axel and Andy seemed to have finished their conversation by the time Doreen laid the bills on the table. "Andy, you better call that organizer fellow back and tell him you want to sell at the horse show after all."

Andy reached out to touch the bills as if they were alien artifacts that might explode beneath his fingers. "How on Earth...?"

Taylor hefted her armload. "You, sir, are an artist of high degree, and I look forward to buying more of your work in the future. I'll put my special orders in after your shows."

Axel beamed at her. "That is so cool. Hey, Andy, do you ever make stuff that will fit reindeer? I've got breed stock in my barn."

"Maybe he can make something to keep alpaca spit from hitting home," said Taylor sweetly.

Axel laughed.

Andy seemed as overwhelmed as Doreen had been. "This is...deeply appreciated."

"Don't forget my offer," said Axel. "You've got my phone number right there. Let's talk soon, okay?"

Andy nodded, unable to find another syllable.

They said their goodbyes and loaded into the SUV. Taylor waved at Doreen, who stood in the doorway, wiping tears from her eyes.

Taylor sank back in her seat. "What wonderful people," she said.

"I know. I really like them, too. And guess what? Andy showed me letters just like the ones that the Shanes got." He patted his breast pocket. "He let me take them after we talked." He turned the car around and moved slowly down the gravel road.

"Yeah, what was your mysterious offer all about?"

"I told him his property was more valuable than he thought, and if it was just about money, I'd rent his land for more than the oil people would give him, and he and Doreen could keep the deed and live there for as long as they want."

Taylor unhooked her seat belt so she could lean over and kiss Axel on the cheek. "That's so cool! You keep doing things that make me love you."

Axel slowed at the end of the driveway and turned to look at her. Teasingly, he said, "I say something incriminating in front of witnesses, but you only say you love me when no one else is around. Should I be worried?"

Taylor took advantage of being stopped to wrap her arms around him and give him a real kiss. "Don't worry," she said, "I'll look for opportunities to say it in front of other people."

Axel hugged her back. "I'll hold you to that. What are you going to do with all this stuff?"

"Use it! And I'm calling the stable manager in New York to tell him about Andy's work, and I'm going to help the Pattersons figure out how to sell online."

Axel grinned. "Excellent." He checked the highway, getting ready to pull out, then stopped abruptly again. "Hey! I thought you didn't have any cash? That's why I paid for all your tack at the Feed and Grain."

Taylor refastened her seat belt and tossed her head innocently. "I spent way more than $800 at the Feed and Grain," she said. "So technically, I was telling the truth."

Axel laughed out loud. "Fair enough. Okay, let's go talk to my cousin. Something in one of Andy's letters made me suspicious."

Chapter Thirty

WHEN AXEL PULLED UP IN FRONT of Thor Security, Rocky the Doberman announced their arrival.

Axel pointed at the dog. His front feet were on the window ledge and every bark left a circle of hot breath on the glass. "That right there is the best security," said Axel.

"Oh good. That means we can have dogs."

Axel felt a tingle upon hearing Taylor talk in terms of "we." He never knew how good that felt before meeting her.

"You're not afraid of him, are you?" he asked.

"No, not afraid. Cautious. After all, it looks like he's on the job."

When they approached the door, a stern male voice ordered, "Rocky, go to bed." Rocky stopped barking and retreated to a large dog bed in the corner of the shop.

Thor didn't have his summer tan yet, but his blond hair and sky blue eyes were as distinctive as ever and his muscles proved he'd worked out all winter. He opened the door.

"Good morning, Cousin." His gaze flicked to Taylor. "What can I do for you? Need security for that house you're building?"

Axel shook Thor's hand. "Not yet, but I will before the summer's over. This is Taylor," he added.

Taylor shook hands as well, announcing, "We're almost engaged."

Axel blushed. Thor grinned. "Have you consulted Axel about that? I thought Lester's drunken wedding toast made you swear off the ladies for the rest of the year."

Axel shuffled his feet. "She's just evening the score," he said, but his tone and expression made it clear how he felt about Taylor.

Thor clapped his cousin on the back, then said, "Pleased to meet you, Taylor. Love your hair. Come on in and have a seat."

The plastic chairs facing his desk made a modern statement in the historic brick building. On the walls, staggered acrylic shelves displayed a large variety of home security devices. On one wall, a TV screen played a film about the joys of knowing your house is protected against any and all dangers. Axel was amazed by how many possible risks were involved in owning a house, but he figured in the security biz, scare tactics were part of the game.

He and Taylor sat down, and Thor took his chair behind the desk.

"Not to sound callous," Thor said, "but I'm surprised to see you so soon after you walked out of that last city council meeting. I had the distinct impression that you were less than pleased with me."

Axel waved that aside. "We may disagree here and there," he said, "but we're family. We both have to deal with the same crazy relatives. I leave that zoning stuff up to you and the city council."

Thor looked hopeful. "Does that mean you're going to accept my offer for your property?"

Axel chuckled. "No, sorry. I really love the place. I can understand why you settled here. But there is something I want to ask you about. It concerns some other property offers." He pulled the Pattersons' letters out of his pocket. "Do you know anything about these?"

Thor examined the letters one by one, reading each carefully and frowning at the signatures. At last, he commented, "Pretty coincidental for people I never heard of to have handwriting that looks like my dad's and my uncle's. I don't recognize the third one, though."

"Your dad? You mean Rudy wrote one of those letters?"

"I'd bet money on it. That's his chicken scratch for sure. And this one sure looks like Uncle Lester's handwriting. What's going on?"

"So you don't have anything to do with the property offers to the Pattersons?"

"I'm stumped."

"How about the Shanes?"

"I love the Shanes. Their daughter is giving up the city life to come home and help them take care of the ranch. I gave them a free security system for their place. Promotional move. They can tell all their friends about it. I even hooked up their barn so they can hear if there's a ruckus out there and check for coyotes. They have chickens, you know."

"Yes, Marigold mentioned her chickens." Axel shook his head. "Taylor says the third letter is signed in her father's hand, even though it's a fake name."

Thor nodded. "I see. So we have three fathers involved in something that they haven't bothered to share with us?"

"It would seem so. Are they all involved in your real estate project?"

"No. Dad—Rudy," he clarified for Taylor, "he's sort of involved. He wants a piece of the action. But Uncle Lester? And this other fellow? No."

Taylor said, "Pembroke Hazen. That's my father's name."

Thor flicked one of the letters with a finger. "They all say pretty much the same thing. Heard you were having financial trouble, thought you might like to make good money. The line about leasing? Call me suspicious, but that sounds like a not-so-subtle oil man fishing for a fracking contract. Who else got letters?"

Axel said, "So far, we're only aware of Lucy Baxter, the Pattersons, and the Shanes. We know you wrote to Lucy, but you signed your real name and your letter was worded differently. The Shanes were visited by a lawyer this morning. The Pattersons also received letters, trying to make the case for a fracking operation."

Thor looked disgusted. "Well, there is oil in Colorado. I just wish Rudy wasn't messing with my little patch of it. Sure, I want to build homes, but how am I going to attract high-end buyers if the town is surrounded by fracking operations and oil rigs?"

"So you agree that they're trying to pressure people into letting them look for oil and gas on their property? But why be so secretive?"

Thor made a rude sound. "Because Rudy doesn't like anyone knowing what he's up to. He's had me talking up the housing idea and egging me on to fight the city council. He obviously wants to keep me busy and keep me from sniffing out his real plans." He glanced at Taylor. "Does that sound like something your father might get involved in?"

"Boy, does it ever. My father loves that sneaky stuff. Especially if he's going to make money." She took hold of Axel's hand and he squeezed her fingers gently. "Axel thought his father sent me out here to seduce him."

Thor looked at her askance. Then understanding dawned. "Oh. That wedding toast again. Well, Rudy told me Lester is fit to be tied that he got grandkids before Lester did." He grinned. A moment later, the grin faded. "Interesting, though. All three colluded to send letters to Eagle's Toe property owners, urging them to sell or lease their properties. But I could have sworn that Rudy was talking about some kind of merger coming up—or was it a buy out?—something about Lester being in negotiations with a New York billionaire."

Taylor nodded eagerly. "Yes, yes, that's what my father told me. He said he wanted me to come out here and get the dirt on Lester by pretending to help Axel write a biography about him." She looked apologetically at Axel. "I'm so sorry, sweetheart."

Axel patted her hand, forgiving her with a smile.

Thor leaned back in his chair and rocked to and fro for a few seconds. "You know," he said thoughtfully, "I've been wondering about my dad's commitment to the housing thing. He keeps saying he'll leave all the planning to me. Hmmm." He tapped his pencil against the desk. "That doesn't sound like our family, does it?"

"No," said Axel. "It doesn't."

Taylor frowned. "You mean my dad is plotting with Rudy instead of Lester?"

"I'm not sure," said Thor. "But if Rudy asked Lester to sign a letter with a false name, Lester would do it. He'd never sign his own name without a dozen lawyers looking into it first, but if it was a fake name, I'm sure he'd do it."

Axel said, "I agree. They fight a lot but they're quick to help each other out. The question is, does Lester know what Rudy is up to?"

"And is Taylor's father involved in their game?"

Taylor's brow furrowed. "Have you ever heard Rudy mention a Pembroke Hazen?" she asked.

Thor stared off into space, looking for a memory. "Does your dad have a nickname?"

"His golf buddies call him Mulligan because he always wants a do-over."

Thor sat up straight in his chair. "Mulligan!? Oh boy, Rudy's been talking up a storm about this big deal he's involved in with a guy named Mulligan."

Axel added, "And Bambi mentioned somebody named Mulligan when I spoke to her on the phone the other day."

Taylor snapped her fingers. "So they *are* all three in cahoots. But why put a listening device on my purse? And why send me out here to dig up dirt on Lester?"

Axel looked apologetic. "I'm sorry, Taylor, but I think your original suspicion was right. I think your dad sent you out here to get you out of the way so he could promote your brother to vice president without having to deal with your reaction."

"What about the wedding toast?" she asked. "Do you still think your father sent me out here to seduce you?"

Thor laughed out loud.

"Hey!" snapped Taylor. "It's possible."

"Sorry," said Thor. "I didn't mean it that way. Who sent you? Your dad or Lester?"

"They arranged it between them," she said.

"What reason did Lester give for sending you?"

Axel responded. "He said he wanted me to create a biography of his life with my mother in time to give it to the family for Christmas. So he sent Taylor out to help me write the biography because I told him I didn't have time to get it ready before December."

Thor nodded. "That part makes sense. Last time I talked to Rudy, he said Lester was feeling his mortality because he doesn't have any grandkids yet and that he's having someone write a book about his life." He cocked his thumb and pointed his loaded finger at Axel. "That would be you, cousin."

"For Pete's sake," said Axel. "It's a miracle we turned out as well as we did because we were spawned from the two most conniving brothers that ever lived."

Taylor got up and stood behind Axel so she could put her hands on his shoulders. "So we think all three are involved in trying to get fracking started in Eagle's Toe?"

"That's what it sounds like," said Thor.

"Okay, so what's the big deal about Friday? My dad said he needed all this dirt on Lester before Friday."

Axel covered her hands with his. "Maybe he's ready for you to get back to New York. Maybe he just invented it as a deadline so you would be able to leave Eagle's Toe. He was pretty upset when he found out we flew your horse out here to my place."

Thor's expression brightened. "No kidding? Sounds serious."

Axel and Taylor shared a look that confirmed Thor's suspicions.

Thor clapped his hands together so loudly that Rocky jumped up from his bed and barked. He pulled a dog biscuit out of his drawer and gave it to Rocky. "That's great," he said to Axel. "Ashley will be so excited. You are going to stay here in Eagle's Toe, aren't you?"

Taylor nodded bashfully. "I've fallen in love with everything," she said. "Axel, the reindeer, the landscape, everything."

"Except the alpacas," Axel teased.

Taylor's phone rang. She dug it out of her bag and covered her mouth with one hand. "It's Daddy!"

Chapter Thirty-One

TAYLOR STOOD THERE, EYES WIDE, wondering what to do.

Axel asked, "Did you disable the location finder on your phone?"

She nodded. "Just like you showed me."

"Then go ahead and answer. But put him on the speaker."

Taylor answered. "Hello, Daddy."

Pembroke Hazen hollered so loud that Axel and Thor would have heard him, speaker or no.

"What the hell are you doing in Las Vegas?!"

Thor raised a questioning brow as Taylor and Axel both stifled laughter. She covered the phone for a moment and whispered, "You were right about the GPS finder."

"Taylor Hazen, answer me right now!"

"I'm in Las Vegas with the man of my dreams," said Taylor, running a finger along Axel's jaw line. "He loves horses. He flew Jackson to Colorado for me, and after we're married, I get to decorate the mansion he's building."

"Married?! Over my dead body, young lady. You get yourself on a plane back to New York right this minute."

Taylor feigned innocence. "But Daddy, I thought that's why you sent me out west. Didn't you and Axel's father put your scheming heads together to make us fall in love and get married? Axel said Lester made a big deal out of him being the next one to tie the knot. So now you both have what you wanted. How many kids do you think we should we have?" She laid it on thick.

"What are you talking about?" sputtered Pembroke.

"Axel wants six, but I don't think my body is ready for that."

Pembroke's voice rumbled with anger. "Taylor Hazen, you are not going to marry anybody until I say so, do you hear me? I sent you out there to get information, and you were doing just fine until—" He left the sentence unfinished.

"Until your listening device went silent?" asked Taylor.

For a moment her father was breathing so hard into the phone, Taylor thought he might be having a heart attack. Then the line went dead.

"He hung up," she said.

Axel finally let loose the laughter he'd bottled up inside. "That was so perfect!"

"You were right," said Taylor. "He was never in on the marriage plan. He just wanted to get rid of me for a while. Maybe you should call your father and find out what's really going on."

"I guess I should. But dang, mailing that plastic tracer to Vegas was a stroke of genius. You have to give me that much."

Taylor giggled. "It really freaked Daddy out."

Axel took a minute to fill Thor in on the tracking device he'd found on Taylor's purse.

Thor grew serious. "Not a bad idea, security wise. There are places in the world where kidnapping is a common way of making money. Sounds like your father loves you a lot."

"I'm sure he does," said Taylor. "He just wants to control my every move."

Axel checked his pockets. "Where did I put my phone?"

"Did you leave it in the SUV?"

Axel stood up to head outside but stopped when he heard his phone's familiar chime coming from the floor under his chair. It had fallen out of his jeans pocket. Axel picked it up and cocked an eyebrow at the caller ID. "It's Uly's wife." Then he answered it. "Belle? What's up?"

"Uly wants to know why there are three private security goons at Lulamae's front door, and why do they keep asking for some guy named Taylor?"

"Let me guess. Your mail was recently delivered."

"Ten minutes ago, in fact."

"Did you find the padded manila envelope I sent you?"

"Yes, it's in my hand."

"It contains a small GPS locater with a listening device included. It came off Taylor's purse."

Belle sounded amused. "Gee, I hope his bag matches his shoes."

Axel laughed. "Taylor is a girl." His voice softened as he pulled Taylor close. "In fact, I'm pretty sure she's *the* girl, if you know what I mean."

"I'm very happy for you and I can't wait to meet her. But right now, would you mind telling us what's going on before Lulamae bludgeons these guys with her cane?"

Axel raised a brow at Taylor. "Do you want to tell your father's hired help that you are safe and sound in Eagle's Toe?"

Taylor threw her head back and sighed like a martyr. "Do I have to? They'll yell at me."

Axel made a face. "Really? You're the boss's daughter. No one yells at the boss's daughter."

Taylor batted her lashes at him. "Can't you do it for me?"

Thor lifted his hands in the air and teased, "See what you're in for, Axel? She has located your control panel and is now pushing all the buttons."

Taylor tilted her head impishly. "Ha, ha, very funny." She peeked sideways at Axel. "Is it working?"

Axel grinned. "A little bit. We should let your dad's goons know you're okay."

Thor added, "Besides, if Lulamae decides to call the police, those bodyguards of yours are in for a world of trouble. Everyone in Vegas knows Lulamae."

Taylor slumped in feigned defeat. "Oh, all right. Give me the phone."

But before Axel could hand it to her, Thor stopped him. "On second thought," he said, "before we give up the game, let me talk to Uly."

Taylor and Axel exchanged curious glances as Axel handed over the phone.

Thor turned off the speaker. "Hello, Belle? It's Thor. How's my favorite sister-in-law?" He laughed at something she said. Then, "Is Uly around? I need to ask him a question." He covered the mouthpiece and spoke to Axel. "Uly and Belle have put down some roots here. They planned to buy property in Vegas as well, but I think—Oh, hi, Uly…. No, don't worry about those guys. They were following a GPS device that our genius cousin mailed to Lulamae's house. Just give them the manila envelope and tell them Taylor is tired of her father tracking her every move….Taylor….She's Axel's fiancée."

Taylor beamed and Axel blushed.

Thor continued, "What I need to know is this. Have Rudy and Uncle Lester tried to pull you into this fracking deal they're working on?"

Whatever Uly said, it had the power to make Thor jerk the phone away from his ear. After a few cautious moments, he pulled it closer, then nodded and grinned. This went on for another minute before Thor could get a word in. "That's what I thought….Sure, you bet. We need to stick together when it comes to Dad." More nodding. He lifted his free hand and made the universal signal for yakking. At last, he said, "Thanks, brother. I appreciate it. Oh, Axel is definitely on our side. He's the one who told me about it." It took several more attempts, but at last Thor was able to end the call and hand Axel back his phone.

"Well?" Axel and Taylor chorused.

"You'll be happy to know that when Uly told Lulamae that Taylor was your fiancée, she invited the bodyguards inside to have iced tea out by the pool."

"Not that part," said Axel.

Thor laughed. "Sorry. You'll also be happy to know that Uly is up in arms and is going to call Rudy right away and tell him to keep his oil-soaked fingers off our little patch of paradise."

"We need to know how many other people our conniving fathers have approached."

"Uly will find out. Rudy can be a force of nature, but not even Rudy can stand up in the face of Hurricane Uly."

Taylor looked from Thor to Axel. "So we don't have to worry about big oil or gas fracking moving into Eagle's Toe?"

"Not when Uly gets through with Dad. I hope your father isn't too disappointed, but his business deal is about to fall through. Big time."

Axel looked pleased. "Now all we have to do is figure out how to help our neighbors so they won't need that kind of money."

Thor said, "Let's get Ashley involved in this part. And the Darbys and the Fineman Wakes, as well."

"The big guns," said Axel. "I can't wait to hear what they come up with."

Chapter Thirty-Two

BY THE TIME AXEL AND TAYLOR had finished talking to Thor, the streets were filling with afternoon shadows.

Thor said, "It must be four o'clock. Are you hungry?"

"Very. And it's almost time to feed the animals."

Axel smacked himself up side the head. "It's a good thing one of us is thinking about them. It went right out of my mind."

Taylor said, "Let's get a snack at The Muffin Man. That won't take long."

"Great idea."

The menu at The Muffin Man had been expanded to offer fresh pizza in the afternoons, and before long, they were seated at one of the little tables with cold drinks and hot, bubbling mozzarella.

"I'm so relieved," said Taylor. "The thought of all this glorious beauty being marred by the search for oil just makes me sad."

Axel's voice softened. "I'm so glad." He caught himself. "I mean, not that you're sad. I mean, the part where you think its glorious. You know what I mean."

Taylor smiled sweetly and sucked on her straw. "Well, the other good news we got today was finding out your father didn't send me out here to seduce you. Now I'm free to actually give it a try."

Axel chuckled. "I guess there's no point in worrying about that stupid wedding toast after all." He glanced around the little shop and held up a finger. "Just a second." He went to the counter, pointed to something in the recently added candy case, then returned to his seat.

His hands were busy under the table for a few seconds.

"What is it?" asked Taylor. "A Snickers for dessert? Isn't pizza enough to ruin my figure with? You have to add candy?" Her tone was playful.

"No, not candy," said Axel. He grew serious. "There's one thing missing." He put his hands on the table. He was holding an unwrapped bubblegum cigar. Very carefully, he slid the paper ring off the gum and held it up. "I know this isn't what most women hope for at a time like this, but it is a ring. We can go to a jewelry store tomorrow. But the way things have been going, what with everyone already saying we're engaged, who knows what other craziness will pop up? So…." He reached for her empty hand—the other was holding pizza—and asked softly, "Taylor Hazen, will you marry me?"

Epilogue

Six months later…

THE BELL OVER THE DOOR OF Taylor's Feed and Grain tinkled merrily when Axel breezed in on a gust of October air. He strode to the counter and leaned across it to plant a kiss on the blue-haired proprietor.

"Hello, my beautiful wife. How is your day going?"

"Great! Even better now that you're here." Taylor came around the counter and returned his kiss, leaning into him and wrapping her arms around his waist.

"Careful now," said Axel huskily. "It's the middle of the day. What will people think?"

Taylor laughed. "They'll think I hit the jackpot," she said. "Any news from Bambi?"

"Yes. She called this morning to let me know she's sent the biography to the printer. Your idea about letting her take over that project was absolutely inspired. She said doing it made her feel like she's really part of the family."

"I'm so glad."

"And I just picked up a box at the post office."

Taylor jumped up and down with excitement. "Your paperbacks?"

"Yep. Turning my book into a romantic comedy was a smart move. Turns out I'm not good at writing about dark dystopian topics. But our sales numbers on the digital version of the romance are really picking up steam."

"Fantastic!" She hugged him again. "How is my horse?"

"You just saw him this morning. Since then, he has demanded room service for his stall and finagled three sugar cubes and half an apple out of me."

"You're going to spoil him," warned Taylor.

"Good. I'm on a roll. I like spoiling you, too."

"How so?" Taylor pulled away and planted her hands on her hips in mock astonishment.

Axel spread his arms. "I bought you a Feed and Grain store, didn't I?"

Taylor smiled and moved flirtatiously down the aisle displaying fly traps and insect repellent. She pulled two traps off the shelf. "We need these," she said sweetly, pushing them into Axel's arms.

Axel grinned. "Romantic. Fly traps."

Taylor continued. "Mr. Carpenter came by this morning. He says he loves what we've done to the place. And I've sold over a thousand dollars of Andy P's Leather Goods today."

Axel watched her with a mixture of love and pride. "Your plan to get him online with his leather work has really turned their lives around."

"And we get first choice of his stock to sell here. I doubled all his prices. He was practically giving it away."

"Strange how things work out, isn't it? Before his accident, he had no idea that an artist lived inside him."

Taylor stopped to help a customer pick out an Andy P dog collar, and Axel admired the new signage and bright, open displays of bird seed, chicken feed, and dog and cat food. He set his fly traps down next to the register and wandered through the store. A large bulletin board at the back was covered with local news and notices of animals for sale.

"Hey, Taylor? What happened to your 'help wanted' flyer?"

Taylor came up behind him. "Don't need it anymore. The Shanes' daughter wants to work thirty hours a week, and Sunny—you remember, Brady's wife, the dog trainer who rescues animals?—she wants to work thirty hours a week, too. So I'm covered. It looks like I might even get a couple days off for myself."

"That's wonderful!" Axel took her in his arms. "Has your father forgiven us yet for getting married in Colorado?"

"I don't know what made him madder, having to fly out here for my wedding or realizing I wasn't asking him to pay for any of it." She gazed fondly at her husband. "Thank you so much for bringing my girlfriends out for the ceremony."

"Hmmm," said Axel, "I think that's only the thousandth time you've thanked me for that little item, but you've only thanked me five hundred times for the Feed and Grain."

"Well, I've got some work to do, haven't I?"

Axel chuckled. "The best part of bringing your dad out here was the way he seemed to love our little piece of Colorado." He looked around the store. "I don't suppose you can leave early?"

Taylor gawked at him. "You are such a stinker," she said. "Until the ladies start next week, it's just me in here and Cody outside, loading bags of feed for customers. I can't shut down in the middle of the day."

Axel sighed. "I knew you were a businesswoman at heart when you convinced Cody his career opportunities would be more promising over here than at the Cattleman's. I just didn't realize how dedicated you would be."

Taylor smiled. "Well, I have to make this place a huge success or my favorite shareholder might get upset." She winked at him.

Axel pulled her closer and planted a kiss on her nose. "That's okay," he said. He checked the time. "I have to attend a Grange meeting with Thor and Ulysses. Our battle to help the local ranchers hang onto their land has struck a chord in Uly, and he and Belle are thinking about teaming up with one of the ranchers to start a summer camp for special needs kids, with Zachary King's help."

"Wonderful! Now go away so I can get back to work." Two more customers came through the door. "I'll be right with you," she called.

Axel lowered his voice. "What about the part where you have to keep your shareholder happy?" He retrieved his fly traps.

Taylor gave him a playfully smug look. "Thanks to Daddy's wedding gift, I can buy out my shareholder any time I like." She walked him to the front door. "Come back after the Grange meeting, okay?" She kissed him warmly.

"I will, and I'll bring dinner from Il Vaccaro." He held her cheek and leveled her gaze so he could stare into her eyes. "Your father really surprised me," he murmured.

"Me, too," said Taylor, squeezing his hand. "And the gift card was priceless!"

Axel laughed at the memory of it. Pembroke Hazen had written Taylor an embarrassingly large check for her wedding gift, and the card had read, "Buy your own lousy Van Gogh."

Axel grew serious. "He loves his little girl," he said.

"Well, I think Lester must have been pretty generous, too," said Taylor. "He was such a good sport about the lying email I sent my dad. When that moving van pulled up in front of the house, I was astounded. Have you unloaded it yet? What was in it?"

Axel cleared his throat and pulled out his phone. "I knew you were going to ask, so I took some pictures before I left. It's still in the van because the interior work on that room hasn't been finished yet. Here. Look." He held up his phone and thumbed slowly from one photo to another.

Taylor's surprise turned to tears of joy. "He sent us a nursery!"

"Yes, and a note." He took a card out of his jeans pocket.

A winged cherub floated on a yellow background. Inside, Lester had written, "Get busy!"

Other Books by Regina Duke

The Wedding Wager (Colorado Billionaires, 1)
The Wedding Hope (Colorado Billionaires, 2)
The Wedding Venture (Colorado Billionaires, 3)
The Wedding Belle (Colorado Billionaires, 4)
The Wedding Guest (Colorado Billionaires, 5)
The Wedding Toast (Colorado Billionaires, 6)
The Wedding Gift (Colorado Billionaires, 7 – Summer 2017)
Colorado Billionaires Boxed Set (Contains novels 1, 2, and 3)
Colorado Billionaires Boxed Set 2 (Contains novels 4, 5, and 6)
Colorado Billionaires 8 Novellas (Contains: *Sunny's Christmas, Krystal's Christmas, Christmas Angel, Love Again, Twice the Joy, Jingle Bell Magic, Jingle Bell Wedding, Jingle Bell Romance*)
Colorado Billionaires Christmas 2014 (Sunny's Christmas, Krystal's Christmas, Christmas Angel)
Colorado Billionaires Christmas 2015 (Jingle Bell Magic, Jingle Bell Wedding, Jingle Bell Romance)
Love on the Lazy B: Love Again, Twice the Joy (Two Colorado Billionaires Stories)
Self-Help for Writers: Being Your Own Cheerleader
My Vampire Wedding
Trickster and Other Stories
Loving the Sensitive Dog

And from *Lovers Lane Romance*

North Rim Delight (Silver State Romance, 1)
The Woof in the Wedding Plans (Silver State Romance, 2)
Calin's Cowboy (Silver State Romance, 3)
Silver State Romance Boxed Set (Contains novels 1, 2, and 3)

If you enjoy Regina Duke's books, you will love Sandra Edwards' romances.

About Regina Duke

USA TODAY Bestselling Author Regina Duke writes sweet romance, cozy mystery, and paranormal. She lives in the High Desert with her three dogs, and when she's not writing she's playing the piano and enjoying her friends. For more info on Regina's books, visit her websites: ReginaDuke.com (fiction) and LindaLouWrites.com (non-fiction).

Visit the author at her author page http://www.amazon.com/Regina-Duke/e/B005KB08YM or email her at me@reginaduke.com.

.

72988105R00088

Made in the USA
Columbia, SC
01 July 2017